THE HARDEST ONES TO FOOL

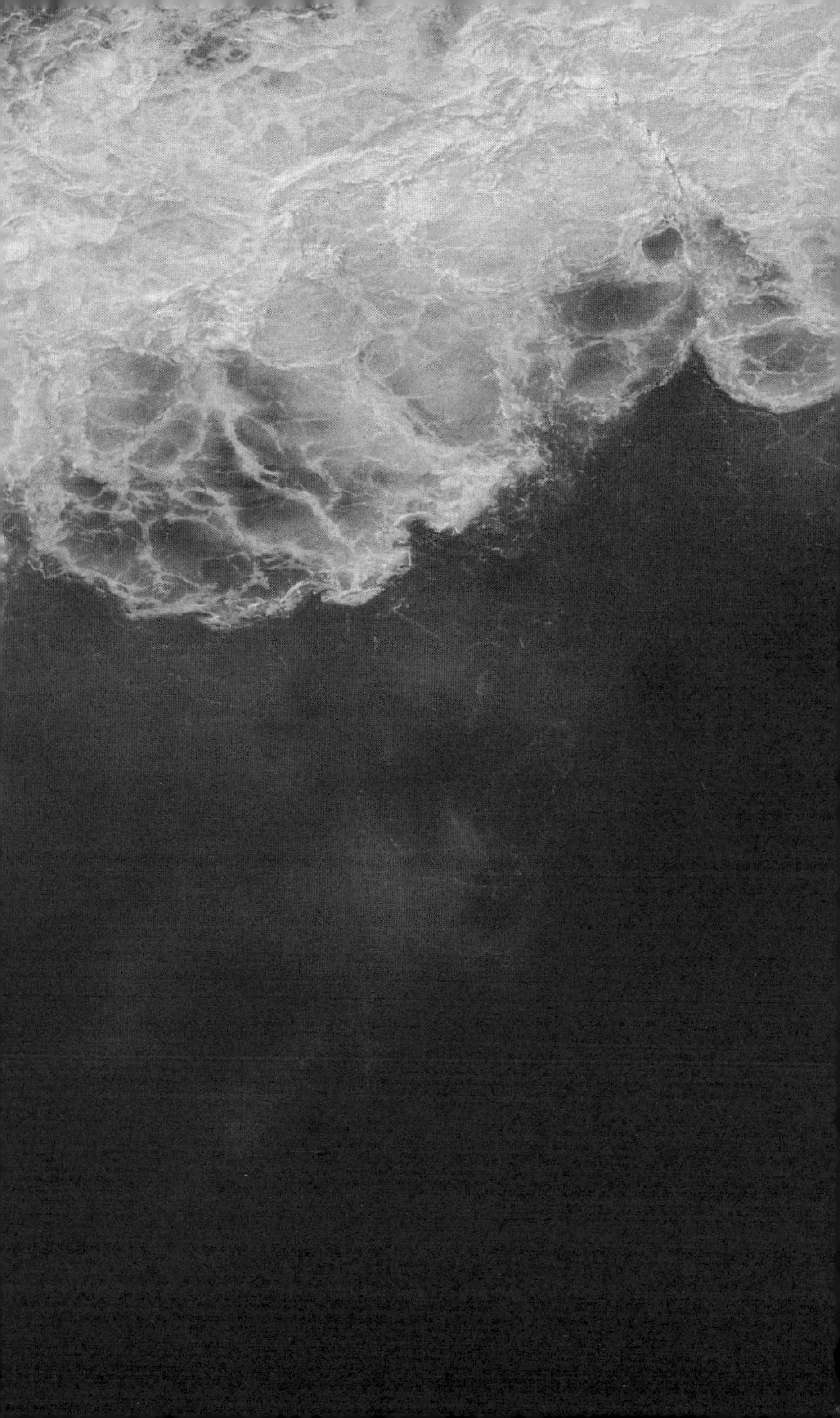

THE HARDEST ONES TO FOOL

Christina Li

Penguin Workshop

PENGUIN WORKSHOP
An imprint of Penguin Random House LLC
1745 Broadway, New York, NY 10019
penguinrandomhouse.com

Photo credits: (front cover) Krapels/iStock/Getty Images, (back cover) vasilyG/iStock/Getty Images, (inside cover) Gojal/iStock/Getty Images, (textures) h2o_color/E+/Getty Images, nico_blue/ E+/Getty Images, stockdevil/iStock/Getty Images, (title page) howtogoto/iStock/Getty Images

Design by Jay Emmanuel

Library of Congress Cataloging-in-Publication Data is available.

First published in the United States of America by Penguin Workshop, 2026

Manufactured in China
TOPL

ISBN 9798217053148
10 9 8 7 6 5 4 3 2 1

The authorized representative in the EU for product safety and compliance is Penguin Random House Ireland, Morrison Chambers, 32 Nassau Street, Dublin D02 YH68, Ireland, https://eu-contact.penguin.ie.

To Joelle and Racquel—let's look at the moon together.

Part One

The Ruse

Chapter One

My mom thinks I'm tutoring right now.

My cover story is that I'm helping some desperate junior with the SAT math section. But the boy I'm making out with on his beige leather couch doesn't actually need one bit of tutoring. Dalton Burke's dad already donated millions last year to his top college (and his backup, just so he could have options). There will be a Burke chemistry wing somewhere at Yale, a fact that this boy in front of me deeply resents. He is independently smart: He's debate team captain, sensational at trivia, and likely the only high schooler in La Jolla who buys and reads actual physical books from the philosophy section of Warwick's and holds intelligent conversations about them. That brilliance drew me to him in the first place. I know he wishes he could just have a chance to prove himself without his parents intervening every step of the way. When he told me that, I had to physically restrain my eyeballs from rolling out of my sockets. But unfortunately, he *is* an incredible kisser, so I humor him. His teeth lightly trace my bottom lip. The room is airy, the windows cast open, warmth beaming down on us. His fingertips run down my arm in a way that makes me shiver. I shift, feeling him press against me, and–

Glass clatters on glass and we jump apart. We've knocked

over a wine bottle on the coffee table. I leap for it, worried I've broken something. The Georgian silver gilt coasters are worth a semester of private school tuition. But the Herman Miller table is unscathed, as are the coasters. The carpet, less so. There's a dried wine stain. I get up and survey the wider aftermath of Dalton's party from last night. Furniture surfaces—armrests, the mantel, the TV console—are littered with empty chip bags and plastic cups filled with alcohol that have been left out overnight. Playing cards lie scattered on the floor. There's a cloying, acidic sweetness to the air.

"We should start cleaning," I say. "Your dad's coming home in, like, two hours. Maybe even less." Depending on how the traffic from the Palos Verdes golf courses is today.

"Ugh, come on, Amy." Dalton leans back into the recesses of the couch and covers his face. "Okay. Fine. Let's do it." He pushes himself up, kissing my shoulder, and then gives me a long, thoughtful look.

I feel suddenly self-conscious. "What?"

He shakes his head. "Nothing. Thanks for helping out."

"Of course." I beam at him.

Combining all the half-filled sticky cups into one revolting cup, I carry them to the sink and pour them out. I paw everything into the trash bag and bring the lamps and the glass vases out from the cabinets. Dalton scrubs at the carpet with some diluted dish soap and water. His thick, wavy brown hair, honey-streaked from the sun, falls in front of his eyes and he pushes it back with his free hand. He's methodical. He's done this before, I know, because everybody talks about the parties at the Burke house on La Jolla Shores, the beach cliffsides a stone's throw away, and also, the first time we met was at his Halloween party. There's no panic. His parents are more absent than most and lean heavily into plausible deniability.

I haul the bag up and tie it shut. "Here."

"Thanks." He sits back and stares at me again with his clear green eyes. His jaw tenses and he tilts his head, the generous sunlight brushing the sculpted, gorgeous planes of his tanned cheekbones. He has something on his mind. Conflict clouds his expression.

Now I'm getting slightly flustered and concerned. "Everything good?"

"Who was that guy you were talking to last night? On the steps?" He nudges his head toward the massive foyer and staircase.

Shit. He's talking about me running into Aditya. Did he see us go upstairs together after? I hope my face isn't red.

"Just catching up with an old friend," I say airily. "We met at tennis camp years ago."

"I see."

He's still looking very intently at me. Dalton's the hardest one of them to fool. He's not letting this go, not just yet. I know what matters to him is not how I answer but my reaction. I keep my head cool. Try not to let my gaze wander up to one of the second-floor bathrooms, where Aditya hoisted me onto the sink counter and kissed me—

"It was good to see him again," I continue. "But I barely know him. We weren't, like . . ."

"I know. I wasn't implying anything."

I hold my eye contact with him for a second more, and then he drops his gaze.

I've passed the test.

I settle onto the couch. He slings an arm around me. The leather feels stiff and cold to the touch. He picks up his phone, where group chat messages are flooding in—from his stoner surfer friends, his debate camp friends. The group chat names are all esoteric. I have no idea how he can manage to keep track of this many people in his life. My phone is silent today. One text from my mom. A few texts from my academic nemesis, the annoying girl from my AP classes who exclusively texts me questions about homework assignments. Two chats I've turned the alerts off for, for now. I'm on Do Not Disturb on these dates. Nothing from Ingrid, but that's to be expected because she usually wakes up late, anyway. I wonder where she went last night. We only briefly crossed paths, right before I ran into Aditya and proceeded to spend my night avoiding people. It was actually a quite hard thing to do, despite the size of this massive house.

I really need to text Aditya and confirm that we're on for Monday. Max, too. I close my eyes, lie back on Dalton's lap, and let the sun warm my eyelids.

I feel something cold settle around my neck, and I jolt. "What's—" My voice softens. "Oh."

"An early birthday present," Dalton whispers in my ear.

My fingers trace the necklace, feeling out a butterfly pendant with jewels on the wing tips, which I'm pretty sure are aquamarine. I don't even need to look at my reflection in my phone to know that it's a platinum chain from Tiffany's. I caught him looking over my shoulder when I pulled it up on my phone weeks ago. I'd only dropped the smallest hints about it. It's his most extravagant gift yet. I gasp with delight.

"Oh, it's beautiful," I murmur breathlessly, staring up into his eyes in disbelief. "You remembered."

I told him this birth date once—and never mentioned it again. I know how he works. He likes to think that he's thoughtful, that he picks up on the details. Dalton Burke, too, loves passing a test. I glance at his phone. "Your dad will probably be home soon. I should go."

"Wait, stay. Say hi."

I shake my head. "I need to go home and pick up some meds for my mom. Want to hang out sometime next week?"

"Of course."

Slowly, I disentangle myself from him. I feel the pendant knock against my clavicle. "I just need to go upstairs. I think I forgot my charger." I pad across the spacious foyer, the unforgiving marble chilling my bare feet. I ascend the stairs and go straight for the master bedroom and into the massive walk-in closet—specifically, his mother's walk-in. Shelves of shoes line my right, an entire row of the same-looking navy blue pumps. Coats hang above me, carefully preserved in plastic dust bags. Pantsuits in every color, so bright they hurt my eyes.

Being Congresswoman Celia Burke must be exhausting.

I carefully root through the drawers. I don't even want to think about how much everything costs, but still, I do the mental math in my head. There's a drawer that's just full of silk scarves. I dig my hand in, deep, and pull out a sheer soft slip of fabric that feels like water on my hands. A forest print, with bright flowers. I think it's Hermès. She won't miss this.

I stuff it in my bra and swipe my phone charger from the bathroom on my way back.

"Got it," I say as I descend the stairs. We hug, and I pull away, and yet again, Dalton stares strangely at me.

Oh my god. What if he's about to tell me he loves me? He is the only one who's held out this long. I bite my lip. "What?"

He'll say it this time, I think.

"What, is it a crime to look at a pretty girl?" He pauses. "If so, sue me."

I blush and press a kiss to his lips, gathering my car keys. I throw him an impish grin. "See you in court."

The ocean peels away from my sight as I drive over the serene hills of La Jolla. I pick at the chipped leather of my steering wheel, this old Cadillac that used to belong to my dad. I tell Dalton that I keep this car for sentimental value because it's the only thing I have left of my dad, which is not untrue. Max has never seen this car because it'll be humiliating for me if he does. I always drive most of the way and then call a luxury Uber at the last mile to drop me off. I keep my window open. There is a clear air to everything around here. It's a little gloomy right now, but it's San Diego weather and I know the clouds will dissipate before noon. A gentle wind, dampened by salt, will pick up from the cliffside and crest toward the water. The cove will fill with kayakers and sunbathing sea lions. I drive a little bit inland, toward my neighborhood. I feel the soft silk of Dalton's mother's scarf around my neck. It feels nice and luxurious and vintage. The resale will go for a high value. I fiddle with the necklace. I'll keep it for a few weeks. I'll wear it to his mother's fundraiser—that art museum gala coming up. Then I'll hack into his email to access the receipt so I can exchange it for something else and sell that, too.

I drive to the Asian market by the freeway and pick up some snacks. Coconut milk for myself, the little packaged pineapple cakes for my mom. When I'm almost home, my phone vibrates on my passenger seat as I roll over a hill. I tap to answer it.

"Hi—Mrs. Mitchell?" Huh. Weird of Ingrid's mom to call.

"Amelia, hi." Her voice sounds strained. "Ingrid's with you, right?"

I sit up. "No. She isn't. Why?"

There is a very long pause.

"I thought she was with you," Mrs. Mitchell finally says. "She said she was going to sleep over at your place, but she's not texting me back. You were both at a party, right?"

Sleep at *my* place? I pull over to the side of the road and snatch up my phone. Our sleepovers are always at Ingrid's. Mrs. Mitchell knows that. Ingrid never made plans with me, and she refused when I asked if she wanted a ride back. If anything, it seemed like she was still avoiding me at the party. Why did she lie? Where the hell is she? My breath picks up. I start to assume the worst and tell myself not to go there yet. "Yeah. We were. But I left early, and she said someone else was going to drive her. Is she . . . not home yet?"

"Okay." I can hear Mrs. Mitchell start to panic. "Okay. Um. Well, she was supposed to come home for brunch with her grandparents. But I'm going to call some of her other friends. Um, Dana, Chris . . . ?"

These are Ingrid's theater friends. I lean back, feeling my heart race. I need to stay calm for Ingrid's mom. But still, a little bit of alarm laces my voice. "Yeah. She's probably with them. Maybe one of them drove her and she stayed over with them."

When our call ends, I just stare ahead for a while. I text Ingrid that her mom is checking in on her before scrolling through the texts she didn't answer last night.

I can't worry. The light is too bright; the sun feels too hot coming in the window. I unmute two chats.

sushi on Mon? Aditya's texted. I autopilot send a slew of kiss emojis back and yes, can't wait.

I switch chats to the one with Max Bracken. ty for being there for me yesterday, he wrote. meant tons

I send a single heart emoji. Ofc. Here if you want to talk.

Location scouting and off the grid to take my mind off things, he replies. But ty appreciate u

Have fun, I answer. Love u.

Having successfully communicated with all three boys I'm currently seeing, I get back on the road. Exhaust kicks into my window and I roll it shut. I pull into the parking garage of my apartment complex. I stuff the scarf into my bag and unclasp the necklace. I haul the untouched SAT books from the passenger seat and climb the stairs before unlocking the door.

Mom's sunk into the couch in front of the TV, a blanket draped around her, napping soundly. It's the only way she can fall asleep these days, watching those shows where couples renovate their massive historic estates in England, looking like they enjoy their restored carved mantel more than they enjoy each other's company. This is my mom's special interest. She got an architecture degree in college—in her past life in China, pre-me. But then she married my dad right out of college and they came here and she never put the degree to use because time passed and a foreign degree didn't really get her anywhere here. Between her shifts at the Granada Hotel, she sometimes wanders the fancy La Jolla open houses on her breaks, takes me to them on the weekends and points out the structural and design details she loves. She's often joked that she's going to go back to school when I go to college because she'll have nothing to do. Then she says she won't, because college is expensive. God forbid she spend any money on herself. There's a wistful hint to her tone when she says it, though. I want to make it happen for her. The money from my boyfriends will help with that.

I also think it makes her a little anxious that I'm leaving for college soon. It's been just the two of us for so long.

I think she's asleep until I hear, "宝贝. How was tutoring today?"

I turn. "It was good."

"Oh—I was talking to my coworker yesterday," she continues from the couch. "I told her you are very good at SAT math. Then I tell her daughter to find you at the library." She waves her phone at me. "I gave her your number."

"Thanks. My uh, list is full at the moment." I pour a cup of hot water and bring it to her.

"Aiyah, don't be so picky. You make an exception for her, right?"

"Hm. Maybe." I don't love lying to my mother, and this is the most elaborate lie I've constructed yet. But I also don't want her to ever worry about me, and so it's better that I don't tell her about any of this. There are my justifications, and I repeat them to myself now: *This money is going to help me with college. This money can support my mom.* Ingrid and I have planned this out so meticulously, and we're determined to see it through.

Ingrid, Ingrid. *Where is she?*

Mom drinks her hot water and curls back into the couch. I should tell her that she should be sleeping on a proper bed after working long, late-night hours as the front desk manager at the hotel, that the lumpy cushions are going to mess up her back, given that she slipped a disc this year—but the couch is her comfort, especially with her TV show. Instead, I kiss the top of her head, give her shoulder a squeeze, and go scrounge together a makeshift lunch of leftover microwaved rice and the reheated egg and tomato dish on the stove. I put the pineapple cakes on the kitchen counter. They'll make her happy later. I head to my room and stow away the scarf and necklace for safekeeping. I've got a mountain of homework that I can't senior-spring my way out of. AP Comp Sci will be a breeze, as will multivariable. I open my phone. Ingrid hasn't responded. I go to Find My Friends.

Ingrid's turned her location off.

This is when I start to get really concerned. She has never, in our entire friendship, turned her location off. She's someone who will stalk *my* location and text me about it. She did a lot of that this summer when I worked at the La Jolla Shores Beach Club. She wouldn't ask where I was. She'd just come meet me.

I call her. It doesn't even ring before going to voicemail. Maybe her phone just died. Maybe she lost it. I should have looked for it in Dalton's house. Maybe she got too drunk and carpooled with one of her friends. From newspaper? From theater?

Just then, I get another notification from the annoying girl from Calc.

I never like hearing from Jacqueline Anh: Editor of the school newspaper, exceptional brownnoser, and thorn in my side. After every test, she texts everyone she knows, checking answers. Especially me, who she's vying against for valedictorian. Even the colleges we're going to are rivals: UC Berkeley for me, Stanford for her. Ingrid says she's not that bad, but she's a staff writer and I suspect that Jackie has personally bugged her phone or brainwashed her for her to say that. I specifically turn my read receipts on for her, just so she can see that I've looked at her messages and refuse to answer them. In this particular moment, my academic rival is the last person I want to hear from.

I look down, ready to leave on read whatever homework question Jackie's sent me now. But then I see what she's texted me, see Ingrid's name, and everything in the world goes still.

CHAPTER TWO

Jackie

Are you here????

Paramedics are pulling someone out of the water and we think it's Ingrid

Things move in camera-like, shutter-like frames. First, I'm in the car. Then I'm racing down the local roads and hurtling straight onto the freeway, my pulse thundering, thinking that I'm going to kill Jackie Anh in class if this is a prank, but hoping more than anything that it is. And then I'm back in La Jolla. Back by the seaside. Parking haphazardly on a street that is filled with cars. Racing up the sidewalk.

I often run here in the mornings, and I know the path to the cliffs too well. I sprint up the hill, past the shops, weaving through tourists lining up for brunch and getting their morning coffee, across the green, and toward the cliffs. A crowd of people has already formed. I cram my way through them. There's caution tape. This can't be good. Is she hurt? I'm going into shock. I see the paramedic trucks and a slow numbness washes over me. *This must be for someone else*, I think in denial. *A surfer, maybe.* A tourist who got caught too close to the slippery rocks. A paddleboarder stranded at sea.

Someone grabs my arm, and I try to shake them off before I realize who it is. I stare into Jackie's wide dark eyes. Her cheeks are blotchy. Has she been crying? In all the time I've known her, she's been collected. Impassive. I've never seen her like this. Her words come out in a garbled rush. "I didn't know who to reach out to, I'm sorry, Amelia, I'm really sorry, I really thought you'd already—"

"It's not her." I'm surprised by my own voice. "It can't be."

But then I remember Mrs. Mitchell's call.

Ingrid's location being turned off.

The crowd is murmuring. I'm seeing it happen. I hear the screams behind me and it's Ingrid's mother. I'm aware of the one thought in my head: *How did Jackie know about this before I did?*

The paramedics aren't rushing. They're not hunched around fixing, saving, doing CPR. Which confirms that I'm too late to all of this. There are no other possibilities. I stare at the vast, unforgiving cliffs. I hear an earsplitting shriek and realize it's coming from me.

It's a body bag. The body bag they're loading into the ambulance holds my best friend, Ingrid Mitchell.

"Just hit her head and drowned," Aditya murmurs, and then shakes his head, running his fingers through his thick dark curls. "Jeez. I wonder if anyone at my school knew her."

He's staring at his phone. I shift in my seat and wipe my sweaty palms on my thighs.

He glances over at me. "Ellie? You okay?"

I answer to my nickname—or, rather, the nickname he knows me by. For all intents and purposes, he thinks I live in North La Jolla and go to Lakewood. I don't know Ingrid. I shouldn't. Eleanor Tsai and Ingrid Mitchell have never crossed paths. "That just sounds horrific," I croak out.

I can't think too much, or I'll remember the scene. I'll remember her mom crumpled in her dad's arms. I'll remember reaching for them, straining, only to be shoved back by a police officer. It was yesterday. Wasn't it? No, today is Monday. This was two days ago. Yesterday was a blur. I'd gone to the police station, scoured the news, anything for any more detail about what had happened. It was said that morning kayakers had found Ingrid's body floating in the cove, just before nine in the morning. The tide had brought her in. I'm disoriented by the conversations going on around me in this dimly lit sushi restaurant. Some big family's singing "Happy Birthday" to the dad, and the harmonization is awful. I look down at my salmon rolls. The smell of raw fish makes me want to puke. The sun is just dipping below the horizon and I can see the brilliant dusk gradient on the cliffs. I feel dizzy, being this far above water. Was this how far Ingrid fell? How did she get all the way from Dalton's house nearly a mile away to the cove?

"I don't know how that could happen to someone."

"Cliffsides are dangerous." He grimaces. "Who knows. Do you think she was, like, drunk or something?" His eyes widen. "Do you think she was at that party?"

Neither of us speaks for a second. Okay. He didn't see me talking to her.

I try to keep my tone light. "Maybe. There were a lot of people." I watch him carefully. "How'd you know about it?"

"One of my tennis buddies. Childhood friends with the guy who threw the party." It's a relief, knowing that he and Dalton aren't that close. He pauses. "By the way, where'd you end up going? I lost you after you said you wanted to go get a drink."

Because I ran into Max. But I can never tell Aditya that. All three guys were at Dalton's party that night. I need to be very, very careful with my stories. But if I'd just been focused on where Ingrid was instead of chasing them all around, maybe—

"I went to say hi to some friends from school."

"Right. But you didn't come back. I texted you."

His gaze meets mine. That's what caught me the first time I saw him from across the library. His dark brown eyes, framed by long lashes, so pretty then and now even more so in the candlelight. I became enamored with the rest later: his strong chin, his unruly hair, his sturdy shoulders, his ears that stick out slightly, his animated excitement about everything. His smile is a prize I want to earn over and over. But right now, he's not smiling. He's pouting, slightly.

He shrugs. "I've introduced you to my friends. Why didn't you? I don't know them."

This is a sticky question. Parents are easy to explain away. I need to focus on school, and my parents have forbidden me from dating until college. But friends? That's a question I've had to think my way out of every time.

I shake my head. "I would have. But I felt sick and had my friend drive me home. Sorry. Didn't mean to leave you hanging."

"Okay." There's a silence. He stretches his rotator cuff. "Are you going to eat the rest of your roll? I'm starving."

Relieved, I push my plate toward him. "How's the shoulder feeling?"

"I'm beat after the last tournament, not gonna lie." He wolfs down two pieces of sushi and the pout dissipates. He's easy to please. I adore that about him. "I think I'm just wrecking it by going too hard in practice. Or maybe I'm taping it wrong. I probably have to hit up the trainer tomorrow morning." He takes a long sip of his lemonade. "You know, if I didn't have this tournament coming up in two weeks, I literally could have just coasted. Maybe I should hold back. I can't arrive at Stanford all busted up before I actually play."

Aditya Kalra, incoming D1 tennis at Stanford. The tennis part was all him, his parents, and the tennis camps they made him go to. The Stanford part? All me. Mostly me. I did tutor for real once. That's why I have all those SAT books lying around. That was step one: getting to tutor Aditya Kalra, rising tennis star, ranked fourth statewide. The next was to stalk his public Instagram and craft his dream girl's profile based on his pictures with his exes. Ellie Tsai is just enough like the girls he dates in that she is tall, smart, and wears tight-fitting athleisure that accentuates her curves. She's not a tennis pro but she can play okay and banter better. (It's true. I played tennis all the way up until I was twelve. Then I had to quit because Mom couldn't afford the lessons anymore.) I would tutor him in AP Calculus and suggest he teach me tennis in return—that was Ingrid's brilliant suggestion. With all this time together, of course, I got him to fall for me.

Ellie laughs at just enough of his jokes. She wins the parents over by telling them she's working on a sustainability start-up that focuses on an AI algorithm to gauge carbon neutrality. Well-spoken enough that his mom approves. Ambitious enough that his dad said he liked me at the very first family dinner I attended. He's even mentioned us dating in college, since Stanford and Berkeley are so close by. Ingrid was elated by this.

I can't think of Ingrid without wanting to cry. I'm supposed to be at a candlelight vigil for her later tonight. I'm giving a speech. Under the table my phone lights up with texts from Jackie, trying to figure out the details and asking me when I'll be there. I have no idea why she keeps texting me. Is she going to be writing an article on the vigil? Documenting my speech? I'm still mad she got to the scene before I did. But of course, the reporter in her doesn't quit. She thinks that everything is a news snippet.

"Ellie?"

I snap back into the conversation. "What?" A new worry surges to the surface—is *he* attending this vigil? Is Dalton? What about Max? It's technically open to the public. If any of them come, I can't give a speech. I can't be there at all.

Aditya nods at someone behind me. A server's coming over, bringing us a slice of cake with a candle on top.

I go still. The birthday I told him was in May. Right? I can't be losing track of details. I was so good at remembering this stuff. Aditya leans in. His forearm flexes as he curls his hand around mine. The candlelight glow is warm on his brown skin. "Happy four months."

Oh, yes. It's our four-month anniversary, and this sweet, sentimental jock has made sure we've celebrated each of the months. The reason why this dinner date was immovable. I bring his hand to my lips and kiss it lightly, beam at him. I look at him with the same adoring gaze as we share the slice of matcha cake, as the bill comes and he pays the exorbitant amount and doesn't break eye contact, as we emerge into the parking lot. It's 7:36. If I floor it on the freeway, I won't be late to Ingrid's vigil.

One more kiss. "I'm so lucky," I murmur against his cheek. "This was so thoughtful. I love you." Even if I was the one who picked the restaurant and planned everything. Words of affirmation. That's his love language. Four months in and I know that well enough.

He kisses me back gently. "Just wait until the promposal," he says. "I've got big plans."

Prom, I think as I get into my car. Another thing that gives me anxiety. What if their proms fall on the same day? I can't be in two places at once. And what does Aditya have planned for his promposal? Is he going to surprise me? Try to show up at my house?

I *hate* surprises.

And if he somehow shows up at the real Eleanor Tsai's house, I'm fucked. Not that there's a chance, unless he googles her address. But he won't, because he's normal and not a weirdo stalker.

I can't believe I'm thinking about stupid prom. I start my car. Before I merge onto the freeway, I pull over. In the gathering darkness, I pull a black sweater over my cute black sporty top. Change from my short skirt that shows off my long legs to a pair of dark pants. And before I pull myself together, I let myself cry the rest of the way and finally become Amelia Wu again, the person who's allowed to grieve.

Chapter Three

I'm late to Ingrid's vigil. I park maybe illegally; the trail of cars goes on, and I can't see where it ends at the Mitchell house. I yank off the false lashes that Aditya loves and hurriedly read through the speech I've drafted on my phone.

The Mitchells have opted for a private family funeral, but the candlelight vigil is for the public. The yard is flooded with pinpricks of light. The crowd is fenced in by cop cars and news crews. Local TV is here, and upon seeing the rolling cameras a hot, sick queasiness overcomes me and my legs buckle. I realize I can't make this speech in the moment her mother's eyes meet mine through the crowd. She pushes toward me. I hug her and she clings to me wordlessly. She feels frail, her curly hair frazzled and brittle against my cheek.

"You're here," she finally makes out, and I echo her words, steadying her: "I'm here. I'm here."

Ingrid's mom pulls me through to the front, where candles are nestled at the base of their eucalyptus tree and crowded on the table. Rising above the candles and piles of flowers is Ingrid in her fancy senior portrait, her deep-set, catlike brown eyes, her soft smile with her perfect Cupid's bow, her heart-shaped face framed by tight reddish-chestnut curls. I want to remember her like this, and yet I keep thinking of the body bag, of the police at the station, telling me how she appeared to them. Shattered collarbone. Lacerations on her cheeks. Fractured skull. A drunken fall off a cliff and carried out by the tide; that's what the police theorized yesterday, that the coroner was likely to rule it as an accidental death. I'm crushed by this torrent of horrific images and flattened into wordless silence. I want to cry. Why can't I cry? Everyone else is. Jackie is over there sobbing so hard, I think she might puke.

Ingrid's mom hands me a candle and I barely register my fingers curling around it. She gestures to the mic. "Go on, honey."

I have to give this speech, even though it's in front of all these people, even though I know news cameras are trained on me and potentially exposing me on TV. I have to do this for her mother; I have to do this for Ingrid. In this moment, nothing else matters. I scan the crowd; it's the people from our high school, the people from her church, her family with her cousins. Everyone's looking at me now. I pull up my speech on my phone, but the words smear into each other and I can't hold the candle and the microphone and my phone at the same time, so I just stand there, facing the massive crowd.

"Ingrid was . . ." I start and then falter. *Was.* That one word guts me. From the front of the crowd, Jackie's looking at me expectantly, her eyes narrowing as if this is something I'm failing because I can't conjure up the words to describe the friend I've known the longest.

I look toward the sky. "Ingrid and I used to call each other on the phone after we came home from school, because it wasn't enough to see each other eight hours a day in all our classes.

We'd invent a secret code, because we thought our parents were listening in on us. This year, I thought the biggest worry in my life was that Ingrid was going to be all the way across the country for college. We had promised to put together a shared calendar once we went away. I never thought there would be a time we didn't walk into school together on the first day, or coordinate our Halloween costumes together based on a clever joke that she'd thought of, or have a sleepover at her house and watch movies, or go on a hike, or just go down to the beach when we didn't have anything better to do." I swallow. "It was hard to accept that Ingrid and I wouldn't see each other every day once we started college. But I didn't . . . I don't know how I'm going to cope with the fact that I'm going to have to live the rest of my life without her."

My body is shivering right now. My throat closes up. I look out at the crowd of people, at the stony faces of the police, and I think of them dragging me back when I was trying to run toward Ingrid's parents. I try to force words out, but it comes out as a croak, and the candle flickers in the wind and goes out. I drop the microphone and I crumple.

And then someone is holding me up, and it's my own mother.

She folds me into her arms. She's short—I take after my dad in height—but I collapse into her, and she rubs my back as my tears burst onto the pleated linen shoulder of her work uniform.

"I'm here," she soothes me.

I cling to her. She must have been on her way to work and stopped by. I didn't even tell her about this. Maybe Ingrid's mom did. My mother hauls me to the side and guides me through the crowd of people, and I sit on the curb and ground the heels of my palms against my eyes as I cry.

"Let's go home," my mom says in Mandarin, discreetly. "I'll call out of work and make you something."

I pull myself together. "No, it's okay."

I look at my mother's face. She's totally at a loss for what to do, seeing her usually independent daughter fall apart in front of her. Worry lines pucker around her lined lips. Her hair is done so immaculately pulled back into a tight bun.

"You can go to work," I tell her. "I drove here. I'll take care of myself."

It takes a while to reassure her before she leaves for her night shift. I linger at the edge of the crowd and avoid the cameras. Maybe there's no point in that; the news has already caught me in a public breakdown. People are going up and giving speeches about what they loved about Ingrid. Her theater friends are talking about how she always brought in her baked goods to test, how she had a crazy good memory and never forgot a step of dance choreo, how great she was at the improv games they played to kill time during tech week. Someone in peer leadership group, a freshman, tells us a story about how kind Ingrid was as a Senior Leader, and how she always took time to listen and give advice to help freshmen adjust to high school, and how she made homemade brown butter chocolate chip cookies and handwrote cards to everyone the first day of school. Jackie is talking about Ingrid's encyclopedic knowledge of old-school rom-coms and how much fun they had during late nights in the *Helicon* newspaper room, preparing the layout of the weekly issue. I chafe at this. Watching rom-coms was always Ingrid's and my thing. We'd marathon them starting over winter break; we used to quote lines to each other. And nobody wants to stay late after school hours on a Thursday night. I had to rescue Ingrid from there a few times when Jackie was holding her hostage over copyedits.

The police are milling about, bored, looking at their feet. This is the time to approach them. I recognize one of them and go straight to him. "Hi. I'm Amelia. I'm Ingrid's best friend. We spoke on Sunday, remember?"

He was the one I provided my statement to that day; I'd shown up to the precinct shaking so badly, I thought I'd collapse. He'd brought me a disposable cup of water, and that small kindness calmed me down enough that I could tell him what I knew about Ingrid and what I knew about the timeline. Now he nods at me briefly. "Are there any updates? Or potential causes of death?"

He glances around. "Listen, there's not much I can share with people outside of her direct family, so I can't say more at this point. But we're working with the family closely to conclude the investigation. There's not much of an update from what I told you."

"*Conclude?* So the case is going to be closed?" I'm stunned. Just like that?

He lowers his voice. "All I'm saying is that several witnesses, including you, saw her consuming alcohol at this party. Underage alcohol consumption is particularly dangerous. Results in plenty of accidents. Some are fatal."

"What? You're *victim-blaming*? Everyone parties as a teenager." Jackie's sharp voice cuts in and I jump.

How did she appear next to me? Wasn't she just giving a speech?

"But how did she end up a mile away?" she continues. "Have we ruled out foul play? Has an autopsy been requested? Can we interview anyone on background today? Also, can I record you?" She has her phone out.

The cop stiffens; clearly, he's rattled by her eavesdropping, too. His whole demeanor changes. Something garbles out of his walkie-talkie.

"Like I said, I can't reveal more details or I'd be violating protocol," the cop says sharply. "The autopsy is for the family to decide. I suggest you ask them. Good night, ladies. I'm sorry for your loss."

I shoot Jackie an incredulous look. "Why were you trying to *record* him? What are you doing here?"

She draws herself up. She looks proud of herself and I feel even more irate. "I was asking questions. Just common ones they ask on true crime podcasts. I was trying to be helpful."

"This is a *sensitive* ongoing investigation and he was literally telling me information in confidence until you appeared, so you did more harm than good," I spit out, jabbing a finger at her phone. Did she record my speech, too? Jackie, I'm less worried about exposing me; her reach doesn't extend beyond the school paper. I'm mostly just furious that she compromised *my* personal efforts. I need to go to Ingrid's parents now if I want more info. "This isn't a fun case for your entertainment. This was my best friend. And you had to hijack it because you—I don't know, want your big journalism break from this?"

Jackie recoils, and it's evident that I've hurt her. I'm smarting with so much pain myself that I don't care. She blinks hard; there are tears in her wide brown eyes. "I was *recording* because I thought it would be helpful, and I want to know what happened to her. You weren't the only person who cared about her." She turns on her heel and walks away.

Cared? I seethe at her retreating figure. All Ingrid did was bitch about Jackie.

"Was her cell phone recovered? Could the police get information from that?"

I'm in the warmth of Ingrid's house after the freezing, misty outdoor vigil, carefully separating the piles of bouquets that people brought, unwrapping them and arranging them on the dining table. The kitchen is strewn with half-melted candles and flowers. We've run out of vases, and so I'm putting them in pasta jars and pitchers. Ingrid would have especially liked this bunch of pink spider mums. I always brought chrysanthemums to her after her *Nutcracker* performances back when she was doing ballet. I arrange them against a cluster of white lilies and ferns.

"It's gone," Ingrid's dad says. "Police never recovered it." He takes off his glasses and rubs his eyes with his hand. He doesn't sit on the couch like Ingrid's mom does, but leans against the armrest of it, his lanky, tall frame practically concave. He's exhausted. "We're looking to request a warrant to collect phone records. But we can only do that if there's an open court case."

"Or probable cause," Ingrid's mother interjects, her voice hoarse from all the talking she's done. She pulls her curly gray hair into a clip and waves at me. "Sweetie, you don't have to do all that. Come sit." She gestures absentmindedly at the armchair across from her.

"But I want to be helpful." And I can't sit with them. I'm going to look at her mom, and I'm going to cry again, and I cannot lose it in Ingrid's house, in front of her parents. It would be incredibly disrespectful. I need to at least hold it together while I'm here. I focus very, very hard on my current flower bundle, trying to wipe my nose with my shoulder. "And they don't think . . ."

"They've ruled it as an accident. They say it's not uncommon for people to fall, especially when visibility is poor at night. The cliffs are structurally unstable and are slippery with the dew and high tide." Ingrid's mom lowers her voice. "And then there's the matter of . . ."

"Of what?"

Ingrid's dad says, "The police wanted to rule it an accident because witnesses said she might have been under the influence."

Ingrid's mom winces. She crosses her arms and shakes her head, chewing on her waxy, pale lips. "I can't accept that."

"I'm just relaying what the police said."

"But it couldn't have been—just *that*."

There is a silence.

Mrs. Mitchell turns to me. "What was she like the last time you saw her? Was she really . . . *so* drunk?"

I set down the flowers and join them in the living room. I have spent so much time in this living room, sitting on the plush carpet, sinking into their couch. Watching Oregon college football on the TV. Scrolling through our phones. Decorating their Christmas tree with ornaments Ingrid brought home from all their family's travels and then spending the holiday with her family because my mom had to work holidays at the hotel. Ingrid's mom reaches out and grips my hand. Her fingers are ice-cold.

"Tell us everything, Amelia. I remember you picked her up around nine?"

I nod and squeeze my eyes shut. "I drove us both there. I think it was around nine thirty. I wasn't drinking that night, but I was prepared to drive her home if she did. But, yeah, we arrived together."

"And did you stay with her at this party?"

I shake my head. "We didn't really hang out much when we got there. She went to her theater friends, whom I don't know very well." I'd tried to befriend them once, when Ingrid first started doing musicals, but I was always seen as Ingrid's tagalong friend, and I always felt anxiety around them, so I stopped. It was apparent that I was the odd one out, even though they were too nice to tell me so. "So I started to talk to other friends."

Making out with Dalton in his room. Talking to Aditya in the stairwell. Hanging out with Max and his friends on the balcony. Placating each of my boyfriends with attention.

"After that, I ran into her once, but she seemed fine. She wasn't really that drunk or anything."

"But she did drink."

"I think so."

"And then you didn't see each other for the rest of the night?" Mrs. Mitchell frowns.

"My mom had accidentally left the oven on before she went to her shift and needed me to turn it off." I hold out my phone and show them the texts from my mom. "So I went looking for Ingrid and told her that I was going home and asked if she wanted to come home with me. But she wanted to stay at the party. She said she'd find friends to drive her home. I told her I'd come back for her if she needed me. And then I went home."

"When was this?"

I sit back and try to recall. "Around maybe eleven thirty?"

"Why didn't she come home with you?"

Why didn't she? That's a good question. "I think she wanted to stay and hang out with some of her other friends." I look at Ingrid's parents. How do I explain the silence in the car? How do I explain this strange tension that had settled between the two of us these past few weeks after what went down at her birthday, enough that both of us felt it, but not enough to be spoken? How do I talk about the slow, condensing fear that Ingrid didn't like me anymore, that she had outgrown me? Dalton's party had been a chance, I'd thought, to have fun together. To make sure everything was all good again. Yet it felt like Ingrid was avoiding me the whole night until I finally cornered her on the second landing and asked her what was wrong, and even then, she barely said anything.

"I texted her asking if she needed me to pick her up." I turn my phone and show Ingrid's mom the texts.

12:09 A.M.

Me

hey you want me to come back?

12:10 A.M.

it's really fine like i can pick u up and drive u home if u want

Ingrid

someone from cast will dd me dw

Hours passed between our messages, and then there was my frantic string of texts the next morning.

I set my phone down in my lap. "I thought someone had driven her home. I didn't think much of it until the next morning when you texted me." I had gone home, slept, and woke up early when I heard my mom come home from her shift. Then Dalton had texted me, saying that I should come over and hang out.

"Why would she tell us she was at *your* house for a sleepover?" Ingrid's mom is grimacing at my phone through her glasses. "We know she goes to her cast parties. We would have picked her up, no matter what state she was in."

"I don't know," I say. It was an unspoken norm that I always slept over at Ingrid's. She had her big room with her lavender walls and plushy carpet and a bed big enough for both of us to sleep on, whereas I only had a twin. Why did she lie to her parents before she even went to the party? Why would she use me as an excuse, and what was she trying to hide? Was she going somewhere, maybe to meet someone? Cody? Come to think of it, her covert situationship didn't show up to school today.

Again, something I need to look into myself. "I'm sorry. I didn't think—I mean, she's gone to parties, right? I've never had to worry. Someone always drives her home." I wring my hands. A heavy guilt knots tightly around my chest. I'm having trouble breathing. "I'm sorry. I should have stayed with her and made her come home with me."

"You didn't know," Ingrid's mom says, her voice hollow. "No one thought this would happen."

Someone doesn't just *die* at a high school spring break party. And of all people, the last person it would be was Ingrid. And she wouldn't just fall. Not when she'd grown up around mountains her entire life. Not when she went on backpacking trips to British Columbia, where her dad was from, and skiing in Tahoe in the winters. Not when she had just climbed Half Dome last spring with her family at Yosemite. I remember a trip they took me on last summer up to Northern California, right before school started. Back then, Berkeley was the dream school for both of us—it was only later that she changed her mind and wanted to go to NYU and our hopes of staying together were crushed. Her parents had met in San Francisco. We were going to go together. We visited the school grounds and pointed out the buildings, our future dorms, where I thought we'd live together as roommates. We hiked up Mount Tamalpais later that day. We stood in the rolling fields, surrounded by tall amber grass, shivering against the settling chill. The sky was seemingly beneath us, like a mirror image, forming a floor of clotted clouds. I looked over at Ingrid, at her curls blowing in the wind, at her serene expression, the freckles I had memorized when we tested makeup on each other in our rooms. There she was, on top of the world and completely at ease.

"Where did she go?" Ingrid's mom asks. "This doesn't seem right. I just know it. Something about this isn't right."

"You think something happened to her?"

No one answers me.

Finally, Ingrid's dad comes over and settles into the couch. "I think we should get that autopsy."

The apartment is empty; my mom is at her shift at the hotel. At last, I can just be alone. I'm used to it. My mom always has her job at night, and my dad, well. I used to dream of him coming home late, so late that I wouldn't hear the door unlock, and I'd wake up and he'd be downstairs in the morning, and everything would be okay with him and my mom. But I know that will never be the case. So I crawl into my bed and cocoon myself in my blankets and scroll on my phone for news of Ingrid. She's made the local CBS station. Flinging my blankets off and stumbling downstairs to the television, I flip the channel to the news. But it's already passed, so I have to go back to my phone. The details around her death are brief; they just mentioned that she fell from the La Jolla cliffs. A shot from the candlelight vigil, and that's it. My speech didn't make it. No one's did.

Broken vertebrae. Lacerations on her face and hands. Shattered collarbone. Bloated body already in the beginning stages of decomposition. A new, horrifying detail emerges from the CBS report on my phone screen: Water was found in her lungs; she was unconscious in that water, alive, confirming the death by drowning. The news anchor is warning about the dangers of venturing too close to the cliffs at La Jolla since they're eroding every year.

It's been so quickly ruled as an accident; that's what everyone thinks. Everyone except Ingrid's parents.

And me.

How did she end up in the sea? Was the tide high enough to sweep her out? Could she have been thrown from the cliff, pushed? Another chilling possibility arises: What if Ingrid had done it to herself, purposely?

I stare at my phone. I am sinking into my couch, shivering despite being wrapped in layers of blankets, when my screen lights up with a call from Dalton.

He'll just call me out of the blue. And I always pick up. That's how we got close, really. I gave him my number—not the first time we met at the Halloween party, but at Warwick's bookstore, over a month later. Ingrid had told me to wait. Dalton lived for the chase and liked girls who played hard to get. So I pretended to run into him in the bookstore. Instead of texting me, he just called. We ended up talking for almost an hour, our thoughts darting around in perfect syncopated synchronicity. He'd told me he had ADHD and anxiety, and how his meds keep him up at night. He told me all about his parental issues, how his mom would leave him at home starting from when he was seven and make him lie to neighbors so they wouldn't report them. I latched on to everything he told me, about his parental dynamics, about his errant thoughts, and seeded it into later conversations. He thinks it's attentiveness and loves it. I chalk it up to having a remarkable memory. I got the sense that he likes complicated characters, so Ingrid and I made up an entire backstory. Adopted, grew up with older parents who died in a small prop plane crash, so I got shuttled around to all kinds of boarding schools on the East Coast until I moved in with my reclusive aunt here in La Jolla. I shared it little by little, so he thought he and he alone had unraveled my complicated origin.

But today there's no message to decode, no hypothetical to unfurl. He sounds frantic. "Hey."

"Hey." I sound like shit. I force my tone to brighten. "What's up?"

"You saw the news about the girl who fell off the cliff, right?"

I open my mouth and nothing comes to me.

"They're saying that people last saw her at *my* party." His voice is quavering. "Do you remember—seeing her at all? Like what her deal was?"

My voice catches. "I—no. There were a ton of people at your party. If I saw her, I don't remember." I pause. "Oh. I'm looking at a picture of her. I think I saw her coming out of the bathroom. The one on the second floor."

"Was she seriously drunk?"

"I don't remember. I think she looked fine to me?"

"I didn't see her. People were saying they saw her drinking

at my party but that she wasn't wasted or anything. And then she walked out to the cliffs and just . . . fell? Slipped and died?"

I squeeze my eyes shut. "Yeah."

"That's awful. That's—I don't know what to do. Do you think I'm at fault here?"

My eyes fly open. He's thinking of *himself*?

"When I host, people always just take care of themselves. If I thought she was in trouble I would have called her an Uber home. But I never even saw her." His voice trembles. "You know how it gets in my house. I barely keep track of anyone but my friends. I don't know if she pregamed and showed up to my party fucked-up, or—like, there is a chain of events, right? Her drinking may or may not have affected the decision to go to the cliffs. Or maybe she was going there anyway. Maybe she was careful, and the cliff just collapsed under her. There isn't a clear causation chain."

Causation chain? He's lost his mind. He's talking to himself. I usually stay on the other end of the line, a reassuring companion, a soothing voice through which to process his spiral. I, as Amelia, am furious. But Amy needs to comfort him. *He's mysterious. Listen to him, find out his deepest insecurities and fears.* That's what Ingrid and I had planned to do. But this wasn't supposed to happen, not like this. We weren't supposed to be talking about *her death*.

Still, I need to keep it together for her.

I exhale through my mouth. "It's not your fault," I hear myself say dully. "It can't be. People host parties all the time. You had no idea."

He whispers, "Do you think the police are going to question me?"

I lean back. "I don't know. If the police do question you, what are you going to say? What did you see happen that night?"

"I was just—I saw you. I was with you, and then you left because your aunt wanted you home early, and then I was just, like, hotboxing the wine cellar. I would go in and out to say hi to my other friends. But that's it. I wasn't keeping track of anyone who was coming in or leaving my party." He pauses. "So I guess I'll just say I don't know what happened. Which is true. I didn't see her at all."

Dalton sounds nervous. That's my first thought. But is it because he was the one who hosted the party? Is he nervous because of his anxiety? Is he telling the truth?

"Did you go to the vigil tonight? I heard her family hosted one."

Will local news air another snippet of the vigil? I hope they don't. I had a visible public breakdown. Will Dalton see me? Aditya? Max? Now I'm a little nervous.

"No," I lie. "I didn't."

"I didn't either. I almost went. But I feel like I should lie low for a bit. I hope they figure out what happened."

Silence lingers between us. He's always good at reading subtext. I hope he's sensing how much of a callous, selfish dick he's being right now. "I hope so, too."

Chapter Four

This week's edition of the school newspaper comes out two days later. The newspaper team still insists on printing physical copies, which usually pile up untouched by the front entrance. Today, though, I swipe one of the last papers in the stack. I stand overwhelmed in the crowd of people rushing to class and decide right then and there to ditch first period. My AP Calc teacher likes me and knows that I don't need to review for that upcoming test because I'm good at remembering all the material. She won't mind me cutting class. I'm sure that the checked-out lacrosse boys who usually cheat off me will. I wander through the school until I find the empty auditorium. I sit down in one of the old plush seats and open to the center spread.

San Diego Community Gathers in Memory of Beloved Student

The picture at the top is of the candlelight vigil. I'm in the corner of the photo, just out of focus. My mom is holding me, shielding me from exposure. The school has finally acknowledged Ingrid, beyond the hushed discussions the Monday after her body was discovered on the cliffs, beyond the teachers sitting us down and telling us that we had counselors on hand and help if we needed it, after which they briskly moved on and assigned a bunch of homework. At least someone has written *something* about her, even if that person does happen to be the most annoying person I know.

Jackie, to her credit, has painted a moving tribute to Ingrid—kind, generous, smart, observant, decisive. She's woven in quotes from friends and family about Ingrid, words from the school community. I'm not one of the people quoted, and that stings. Jackie didn't even ask me; she just butted in on my conversation with the cop. Actually, maybe she did text me last night, asking if we had time to chat. I just ignored her.

It's annoying that I wasn't included but people whom Ingrid disliked were. There's a quote in here from a girl who'd bullied her on the JV poms team. Unbelievable. This girl, who invited the whole team except for her to her fifteenth birthday party, is now trying to suck up to the school paper about how close she was to Ingrid? I really want to complain about this with Ingrid herself, but of course, she's dead.

At least I can hold her grudges for her.

Jackie writes:

La Jolla has lost a bright, vibrant, beloved member of our community in Ingrid. She was last seen alive at a spring break party in North La Jolla, allegedly hosted by a peer from St. Anthony's High School. Her death has been officially determined an accident, but police have not ruled out foul play. Her family is currently looking to open an investigation into her death with the Northern San Diego Police Department.

Right. The autopsy. How long do autopsies take? Days? Weeks? Could we not get definitive answers for months?

Just then my phone buzzes with a text from Max. I chew on the inside of my cheek and open the text.

Max

lfg just scored an invite to the time travel premiere

Be my date? tomorrow at 6 but traffic will be BAD so thinking of heading up around 2ish

He sends a screenshot of the invite details. It's a time travel romance movie. Oh, fun. The star is an indie musician darling who's just broken into acting—Adaline Chen. I used to love her music. If I go to this, I can meet her. I'll also get to be in Los Angeles, catapulted into Hollywood. I'll get to walk the red carpet on Max's arm in a shimmery dress. For a moment, that tiny pinprick of happiness permeates everything else. I cling on to that small joy for now.

A 2 p.m. departure means I'll have to cut my last two classes of the day. But when have I—sorry, excuse me, *Mia Leung*—ever cared about classes? I reply immediately, I'm there with the black heart emojis that he loves.

want me to pick you up? I know ur parents are strict . . . but I can pick u up from school?

I hurriedly shoot back, that's okay, I'll come to your house and we can head out from there.

Max

Cool come to mine at 1:30

I can get out of my classes, no problem. I just have to fake some kind of medical document. Or maybe I can say it's because of my grief. I don't even need to fake the fact that I can't function in school because of this. I just can't. The classes blend together and I try to listen for the bell each time to signal my release. My teachers' glances linger on me a little too long, and I see the pity in their eyes.

I put down my phone. The lights in this empty auditorium have dimmed, and it's dark. The only thing lit in this cavernous space is the lone spotlight, shining down on the dusty, scratched wooden stage. I've seen Ingrid on this stage so many times, ever since she dropped poms and picked up theater sophomore year. Ingrid was going to be Persephone for *Hadestown* in this year's musical.

I look back down at the article. I text her mom a picture of the school paper. Her mom replies immediately with a series of heart emojis.

Me

Saved you a copy.

Mrs. Mitchell

Thank you, sweetie. Appreciate it.

Saw there is an open investigation with the police of suspected foul play?

We hadn't talked about this on Monday.

Mrs. Mitchell

Not ruling it out. The deputy says there's an uptick of drinks being laced. Her dad and I want to get some kind of toxicology report.

Me

That could be helpful.

Would be nice. Just so many unknowns around that night and not enough info.

I feel the guilt seep in. There are unknowns because Ingrid and I got separated.

The bell rings and I startle. AP Lang is next. We're starting *Macbeth*. I can't do it. I don't have it in me. I can't stop thinking about Ingrid and running through possible autopsy results. I shift my backpack and a piece of paper flutters out with the school counselor's number on it. I stare at it and know what to do next.

I've never been to the school counselor. Her photo on the school website reveals a severe expression framed by a bob and glasses, kind of Edna Mode-ish. Originally, I had just wanted to get out of class. But now it is dawning on me that I do probably need this. It's probably healthy to talk to someone about Ingrid, although I'm scared that if I start talking about her, I'll completely break down. That's what happened at the vigil. I feel clammy and like something is stuck in my chest when I walk past the principal's office on the way to the counselor's. I almost turn around. I don't want to cry in front of strangers again. Maybe we can just sit in silence.

The principal's office door is ajar. He's lecturing someone right now. "This is a *sensitive* topic. You should have run it by the school administration first."

"I wanted to write something. I was telling the truth. Isn't that allowed?"

Is that *Jackie's* voice? I stop.

"Of course it's allowed. You just needed to run it by us first. Do you understand? I know she was your classmate and friend, but there is an order to these things. Especially for a school-wide publication. We want to have unified messaging about this. Talking about the police investigation? That could open us up to all sorts of liability. What were you thinking?"

There is a long silence. I barely have time to retreat before someone yanks the door open and I come face-to-face with Jackie.

Her eyes are puffy, and her nose is red. She's been crying; she catches my eye and swipes quickly at her cheeks. I look at her in curious shock, and then at the principal, this balding white man who's glaring at us with his arms crossed.

"What are *you* doing here?" Jackie asks. Before I can answer, she roughly pushes past me.

I can't even pretend like I didn't hear them. I duck away to avoid the ire of the principal and run into the counselor's office.

Copycat Edna Mode, LCSW, looks up from her phone, where she's been playing a game.

"Hi." I hold up the scrap of paper. "I'm Ingrid Mitchell's best friend. I want to talk to you."

She immediately straightens up and puts her phone away. "Of course." Her voice is soft and soothing. "Please, have a seat."

She looks at me with big dark eyes, bug-like through her glasses. "I'm so sorry about your loss, Amelia. How are you holding up? I can only imagine the pain you are in."

"I, um. I don't believe it. That she's . . . dead." I blink. "I just can't wrap my head around the fact that it's permanent, you know? I keep thinking this is just something that I have to bear . . . today, but tomorrow we'll reset. I'll wake up and we'll get to start over again and she'll come to school and everything will be back to normal." My voice has become high and strained. The room is becoming blurry. Automatically the counselor holds out a tissue to me and I take it. *She is a safe person*, I tell myself. *She is a person I can cry to.* "Except . . . it's not. I have to wake up with this . . . horrible dread that she's gone." I want to throw up. "This is how it's going to be forever."

"This was so sudden," the counselor says. "And it's such a tragic accident, too. It's jarring because it's so unexpected. But it's very clear how much you cared about her."

"I did," I whisper. "I still do."

"I understand this is a very difficult time. I'm here to listen."

I want to say more but I can't form words. I'm taking in very shallow breaths. "I'm sorry. I just—feel like I'm going to throw up."

The counselor slides the trash can over to me. I heave over it, but nothing comes up. My cheeks are burning now, as is my forehead. There's no way I can go to class.

"You can sit here as long as you would like, okay?" the counselor says. "And I don't do this often, but if you need me to tell the nurse to write up a note to let you go home, I can do that, too."

Gratefully, I accept.

Chapter Five

The next day, I'm at my third boyfriend's massive backyard, on the other side from the pool, looking at a blindingly shiny bronze apple that is twice my height. There's no explanation for it. I can't tell if it's the ugliest thing I've ever seen or if I just have severely unevolved taste. I've also been in distress as of late, so I might not be fully appreciative of the arts, or at least Max's backyard art.

Max's stepmom seems ecstatic about it, though.

"It's called *Forbidden Fruit*," she says in a reverent murmur, tossing her long dark hair over her shoulder and holding her beloved Persian cat, Cassandra. "I got it specially commissioned. What do you think?"

I clench my jaw. It doesn't matter. None of this matters. But I have to keep up this front for Ingrid. I need to effortlessly infiltrate Max's life, and cooing over his stepmom's hobby is a part of it. "It's beautiful," I manage. "It's like—a mirror."

Max's stepmom beams at me with her perfectly surgically lifted cheekbones. "Very astute. It's said to symbolically reflect back one's true self and desires."

"I love your taste in art," I fawn, making my voice extra syrupy. "I wish I had an eye for something like this."

"This is cool, Laurel," Max says. "It's sick."

Maximilian Bracken—yes, of Bracken Pharmaceuticals fame—likes calling his parents by their first names, which is a thing I have yet to wrap my head around. Not that I'm a stickler for filial piety or anything, it's just strange. Maybe it's a white-people thing. Maybe it's a kid-of-a-billionaire thing. Whatever it is, he can truly do whatever he wants. Sure, you can address your parents like they're your friends. Sure, build a big bronze apple and a pool long enough to do laps in. Sure, you can have a wine cellar you can get lost in and have heated floors throughout the house and a barricade of electric vehicles in your front driveway. Go nuts! Max calls them decoy cars because of their tinted windows, as if they're spy cars. Sometimes he takes one of them out for a spin.

"I was consulted during this whole process," Max's stepmom says excitedly. "I have pictures of the sketches. Do you want to see?"

"Later," Max says. "Mia and I need to dip or traffic's gonna suck."

"Oh, sure," his stepmom replies. The cat emits a concerningly husky meow and tries to wriggle free. "You guys look *gorgeous* together. And that is just the most stunning dress, Mia. I love the shoes."

"Thank you, Mrs. Bracken." I'm draped in a backless pale apricot Bottega dress that clings to me like water, held up by a chain-link halter whose intact price tag has been discreetly tucked into my bra strap. A gold herringbone necklace that I swiped from Dalton's mom's closet weeks ago that I swear I'm just borrowing for the moment. Gold pearl drop earrings from Five Below, but they blend in. The stars of the show are the

Prada kitten heels whose monthly payment cost me my credit card limit, and that I can*not* get a single scuff on because I have every intention of returning them tomorrow, shoes and dress and all, like a Nordstrom Cinderella.

"Okay. Ready?" Max starts to head in.

I follow him to the kitchen. Suddenly, I pat myself down. "Oh. I forgot my bag at home."

Max lets out a sigh and runs his hands through his sandy-blond hair. "Are you serious, Mia? We're going to be late."

"Wait, take one of mine," his stepmom offers. She sets the cat down, who darts away, and goes up the stairs. She emerges shortly with a small black crocodile leather purse.

I look at it for a second. "Oh, chic," I say calmly, as if I have a thousand of these at home. It's so tiny it's a struggle to fit my phone inside. "Vintage Vivienne? I love it."

"Her 2005 collection," his stepmom says, brightening now that her fashion taste has been acknowledged. "I remember wearing it to premieres back in the day. Now she just gathers dust in my closet. But it looks so nice on you. You should keep it if you want it."

My eyes widen. I could resell this for hundreds, put it toward my mom's college fund and my secret bank account with Ingrid. "Are you sure?"

"Of *course*," Max's stepmom insists. "She deserves to be in the spotlight again."

I look at her big blue eyes set against her forlorn expression, and I see her revived by remnants of this old life of hers. Max's stepmom was a fun Google rabbit hole to fall into. Laurel Bracken (née Pietro) once had an entire exciting life back in New York

City, where she was working as an auctioneer for Sotheby's and running the city as a total it girl. But she happened to sell a stained glass piece for millions to Max's recently divorced dad just a few years ago, started dating him, and now she's given that whole life up to be here, at the edge of the world in the beautiful, sleepy, sprawling hills of north San Diego, bored out of her mind and blissed-out on anxiety medication. But it works in my favor. She's easy to read and desperately lonely. Butter her up enough and she'll just start giving you stuff for free or inviting you to drink fancy wine with her by the pool.

"Ready, babe?" my boyfriend asks.

I straighten up. I grin at Max, who threads his hand through mine. I take a picture of us, post it to my Stories (or, more accurately, Mia's Stories), tag him. For a moment, armored with my designer clothing and a coquettish smile, I have effortlessly metamorphosed into Mia Leung, billionaire heiress. This is just another Thursday. "Let's go."

Every time I end up on a red carpet or a public event with Max, I always get scared. Every click of a camera feels like a splintering of my cover, another exposed risk.

But I always remind myself that the risk is controlled. It's always my fake private Instagram tagged in photos. And I highly doubt Dalton or Aditya are lurking around Getty Images or Pop Crave.

Besides, I need to exude confidence. Mia Leung has no problem with this; she models for *Vogue Singapore* in her free time. I face the cameras with a bored, arrogant tilt of my head and purse my lips in a discreet smile. The flashes are blinding me and I'm tearing up, so I break my blasé character to turn and grin at Max, admiring the floppy, sandy-blond curls that he's carefully gelled back, his big brown eyes, his air of certainty. He grins at me with a slight, endearing gap in his teeth. His hand tightens around my waist and rubs my back. He pulls me to him, and I melt against his body. The photographers capture it all.

Max loves having a shiny thing on his arm, Ingrid told me, and so that's what I've become. A muse. Someone visual, arresting, cinematic, aesthetic, fascinating. We could tell from the way he photographed all his ex-girlfriends on his film-camera Instagram that Ingrid discovered back when she interned with Max's dad over the summer at Bracken Pharmaceuticals. Bright outfits, gold earrings, starlit smiles, windswept hair.

I think of the first time I captured his attention at the local San Diego film premiere and press tour stop for *Carry Us Home*, a film adapted from a bestselling book. Ingrid was able to get us in because she was writing a feature for the Arts and Music section of the school paper. I'd borrowed her fancy Reformation dress she'd worn to a cousin's wedding. I sidled up to him as we were waiting in line for refreshments, convinced him that I was the niece of the author, Tom Leung. Recalled the plot points from the book with startling accuracy; tossed in a couple of stories about how I grew up in a gated community in Hong Kong, how I went to international schools in Indonesia and Shanghai, then British boarding school; the polo star I'd dated; the heartbreaks I'd experienced in the wake of the move to San Diego to stay with my American cousins to acclimate to the country before I enrolled in college. There are kernels of truth. My mom is Chinese Indonesian (with extended family in Shanghai and Hong Kong), and I *do* have a very distant uncle who got rich manufacturing badminton equipment. But a scan of a *Financial Times* article listing the richest Asian entrepreneurs, a few expanded lies connecting myself to the tycoon of household wares on that list, a half-baked transatlantic accent, and that was all it took. Mia Leung strutted out of my brain, Athena-like, with clearance into the life of Maximilian Bracken.

Ingrid and I loved coming up with *that* storyline.

Thankfully we are ushered off the red carpet, where I regain my normal vision. Max leans over and points out a small man who looks like he's being swallowed up by his suit. "That's *him*. The director. Russ Carlson. He's brilliant."

We spend the next hour trying to break into the conversation, to no success, and then it's time for the screening. My phone's flipped over, but I still see the outline of the glow as it lights up with notifications throughout the title sequence. Shit. I forgot to turn on Do Not Disturb. I try not to fidget through the movie and barely register what's happening. Something about a couple who can travel through time, but I'm not paying attention because my eyes are glued to my phone. I know it's about Ingrid.

The credits come up and I mumble something to Max about needing to pee and bolt for the bathrooms. In the stall, I finally open my phone.

Turns out, it's just texts from Aditya about his tennis game that he's nervous for. I roll my eyes and muster up the pep to send back words of encouragement and a bunch of emojis. Another text from Jackie, asking if I've done the active reading of the first chapter of *Macbeth*. Enough screen time. I look up at the ceiling. My head is starting to ache. I'm pretty sure my feet are blistering. I grit my teeth and walk out to the sink, where I examine my makeup next to a girl who's accumulating a pile of tissues. I look at her in concern, and realize I've been staring for maybe a little too long when she asks, "You don't happen to have any hydrogen peroxide on hand, do you?"

She turns and I realize I'm face-to-face with indie-musician-turned-movie-star Adaline Chen, clutching her ear.

I look down. "Sorry. Couldn't carry any with me."

She looks at my bag and laughs. Her speaking voice is low, a far cry from her angelic falsetto. "My purse can't fit a single thing, either. Why do designers make them so tiny?"

"It's, like, for dolls." I nod at her ear. "Is it infected?"

"Yeah. I got my double piercing on Tuesday. Bad idea. The tattoo parlor was kind of shady, but my friend made me do it with her, and now I'm going to bleed all over everyone at my first film premiere."

"We'll fix you up," I reassure her. I reach over and dab some warm water on a tissue. "Can I?" I hold it to her ear. I'm way closer to a celebrity than I should be. She's disarmingly pretty—just as beautiful as she is on social media, with smooth, dewy skin and doe-like eyes—in a way that makes me slightly dizzy to be in her vicinity. She's shorter than I thought she'd be, but then again, most everyone is short compared to me. More nervous looking. I gently apply pressure to her ear. I did this once, when Ingrid's piercing had gotten infected and she'd run out of her Claire's solution. There's a flutter in my stomach.

"You were great in the movie, by the way," I tell her.

Adaline breaks out into a smile. "Really? I kept my eyes closed half the time. I couldn't watch myself. I just start hating the way I talk . . . and look. You know?"

I examine her delicate, poreless face and attempt to believe her. Okay, more importantly: She thinks I'm important, too. She thinks I'm *famous*. "It's like that for modeling shoots for me," I say. "I can't look at myself. I just start picking out all the flaws."

"Oh yeah." She lets out a huff. "Don't remind me. I have a "24 Hours With" for *Vogue* on Monday."

"Ugh, *Vogue* is the worst."

"Really? This is my first time with them."

"So fun. But exhausting. They don't give you a break. And they're, like, *so* particular with your look." Are they? I'm talking out of my ass at this point. But who's going to fact-check us in this bathroom?

"They're going to give me so much shit for showing up with an infected ear."

"Hang on." I press for a few seconds and then remove the tissue. Miraculously, no blood emerges. "There. It's just a little red."

"My lifesaver," she says. She scrutinizes me and her eyes narrow. "So, you model. Do you act?"

"Not yet. Dying to, though." I'm discovering all kinds of things about my alter ego in this conversation.

Her gaze drifts down to my collarbone. "You're really pretty. You could be in one of my music promo videos. Hmmm . . ." Her hands snap to her bag and she fishes out her buzzing phone. Adaline lets out a huff. "My publicist is looking for me." She touches her swollen ear. "Okay. *Thank you.*"

She drifts out of the bathroom. I stare at my bewildered

expression in the mirror. Of course, the three boys I'm toying with have complimented my appearance before, even if I make it easy for them. Ingrid did, too, although her compliments mostly stemmed from what I had that she was jealous of: my straight hair, my long legs, my clear skin and effortless ability to keep a tan. We used to sit on the floor in her room and trade compliments. Ingrid would go on about every perceived flaw about herself while I reassured her. I've never really gotten these compliments from a stranger, though, much less a celebrity. Now, when I look in the mirror, instead of picking at my ears that stick out a little, or my lack of eyebrows, or the long nose I inherited from my dad, I see my sharp cheekbones, my full, lined lips, the gleam in my eyes. What makes me beautiful in this moment? This heavy makeup? Is it the fact that I'm draped in designer clothes? The glamour of this confident persona I've made up? There is a flush in my cheeks, an alluring expression that exudes an enigmatic charm. I laugh a little, and then immediately compose myself when someone else enters the restroom.

I'm about to leave when I notice the earrings by the sink bowl. I know they're Adaline's. They feel heavy in my palm. Diamond drop earrings. Without thinking, I deposit them in my teeny handbag. If I see her, I'll return them to her. If I don't, they'll be my little souvenir of the night to remind myself that it all happened. Now I'm daydreaming about being in one of her promo videos. I really *cannot* do that, because she's a global superstar who has close to a million followers, and being in something that public really *is* flying too close to the sun. But I can fantasize about us walking the red carpet together and having pizza afterward in the luxury of our splashy hotel rooms, her flying me around the country to her concerts and inviting me to her very cool Hollywood parties.

I'm still floating when I run into Max in the lobby of the theater. I breeze over to him and press a kiss to his cheek. He seems annoyed. "Where were you?"

"Bathroom. Helped Adaline with an earring situation."

His eyebrows fly up at the name. *"Chen?"*

"Yeah. We had a real moment in there. She called me pretty and wants me to star in her music videos." I nod toward the crowd. "How'd it go? Did you get to talk to the director?"

He's tight-lipped and shakes his head. Strands of his blond gelled hair are starting to fall into his eyes. "Let's get out of here."

I follow him out. "What's wrong? What happened?"

"He wouldn't even give me a second of his time. Just blew me off. Sure, it's one thing if he isn't really talking to people today, other than press. But, like, bro, do you not even *remember* us meeting at South by Southwest last year?"

I totter after him. My heels are killing me now. "Just email his assistant. I'm sure he'll remember you if you write a nice note."

He fumes. I should know well enough by now that he's not the type of person who interacts with *assistants*. We reach his car and just sit inside it for a moment, in silence. I reach over and clasp his hand and rub my thumb across it reassuringly. "At least *we* had a cute date night."

Max turns toward me, and his pout relaxes, just a bit. "And I had the hottest girl by my side."

He kisses me slowly. He's a little sloppier than Dalton, more forward than Aditya. But he kisses with an urgency that makes me lightheaded. And he's got the most amazing, jacked, brawny arms from all those years of playing rugby at boarding school. He pulls me in and locks me against him as he deepens the kiss. "You looked so pretty on the red carpet tonight, babe. I mean, look at you. I'm going to have to fight an A-list actress for your attention." He kisses me again. "Just kidding. I don't fight girls."

I laugh against his lips. I know part of him is a little annoyed that I befriended Adaline while he got snubbed, so I soothe his ego. "Don't have to. I'm all yours."

He *loves* hearing that.

Suddenly he stiffens. I pull away. My phone's lit up in my lap with a message from Ingrid's mom.

Mrs. Mitchell

Police want to close the case. Just talked to Jackie. We're officially requesting an autopsy for Ingrid with the medical examiner.

I snatch up the phone. How did Jackie infiltrate this? For a moment, I'm so overcome with confusion that I forget there are two people in this car. I look up. Max isn't speaking. He's just staring at me. Did he read the text? It doesn't matter. He saw who it was from.

I should have put my phone on Do Not Disturb. I've been slipping lately. Unraveling in these tiny, careless missteps. This can't keep happening.

"Oh, this—it's about Ingrid Mitchell, you know, this girl—"

"Yeah," Max says faintly. "I saw the news. She was the girl who fell off a cliff, right?"

I wince. "Yeah." He's still staring at me weirdly, so I scramble for an explanation. "Her mom . . . well, our moms know each other, so she's just been updating me."

Max takes a long time before he speaks.

"Yeah," he says at last. "That was really sad."

I watch him carefully. But he doesn't say much more or question me. Maybe any grievances about the movie premiere seem insignificant compared to this. He starts the car without another word.

"I just don't know what to do after the wedding, you know?" Max whines on the drive back. "Therese is guilt-tripping me to join her in the Alps because Marco has a summer house up there, but Laurel wants me to go on a yacht trip with Peter around the Mediterranean, which honestly sounds more exciting to me, but also, there's a fifty percent chance Peter flakes and Laurel just spends the entire time treating me like her therapist."

Max is testing the limits of the Los Angeles freeways. Also, my patience. I can't tell which is a worse way to go—dying in a fiery crash because Max doesn't use his turn signals half the time when he merges lanes, or withering away inside, listening to him complain about choosing between two European vacations this summer. My brain is glitching, between listening to this and thinking of Ingrid. Thinking of the autopsy. They'll carve into her body and take it apart and stitch it back up. They're going to run tests on her tissues and organs.

"Yeah," I try to say in my most sympathetic voice. "It's tricky."

"It's stressing me out. Maybe I should just not pick a side and go backpacking with my buddies. Nate said he'd come to Thailand with me." His eyes widen. "Oooh, we could make a pit stop in Indonesia. Like, Bali! Do you think we could hang out with your family?" He peers over.

"Babe." I clutch my armrest, sweating through the dress I have to return tomorrow. I imagine my body being crushed by the median. I also imagine him pulling up to the gated complex of the billionaire I've claimed as my uncle. "Eyes on the road."

"Sorry." Max careens back to the middle of the lane, and I lose another two years off my lifespan. He drives in silence for a while. "You seem quiet. Are you okay?"

"Yeah," I say. "I'm just . . ."

"Processing the Ingrid news. I could tell." He pauses. "Did you know her?"

His hands are tight around the steering wheel. He's speeding. The car is so low to the ground, I can feel the vibrations of the engine.

"Not really," I lie. "Our moms just go to Pilates together."

That's a thing moms do, right? I keep myself perfectly still. I can't blow my cover when I was already so dangerously close to the edge. Why did Ingrid's mom talk to *Jackie*? Sure, Jackie interviewed them for her memorial piece on Ingrid, but now she's advising them on the case, too? I guess she really does care. I still think about her being trapped in that principal's office, crying while he berated her. To be honest, I do feel bad for her.

"People were saying they saw her. At the St. Anthony's party we were at." I have a thought. Dalton didn't see her at the party, but maybe Max did. Maybe he can help put together the spotty timeline. "Did you see her? Do you remember?"

Max squints. "I think so," he says slowly. "Her face looked familiar to me. I think it could be the girl my buddy was flirting with. We were all playing stack cup together at one point."

I sit up. She was talking to one of his friends from Day? "When was this?"

He sucks a breath between his teeth and effortlessly weaves between two cars. "I don't remember. Not super late? Like an hour after I got there?"

So around eleven. I file it away mentally. "And you didn't see her after that?"

"I don't remember." He shakes his head. "It got so crowded. I just remember being with my friends, and then I hung out with you, and then you kind of . . . disappeared? Speaking of, where'd you go?"

"Oh, yeah." I was back with Dalton at that point, upstairs. Before I left. "I had my mom pick me up. I was feeling kind of sick."

"It was that stale whiskey, huh? I had that, too. I felt like shit the next day."

"Must have been."

"Maybe she had too much of that." His hand tightens on the steering wheel. "Went for a walk by herself for some reason. And just . . . fell." He pauses. "You think her family thinks something's up?"

"I don't know. They probably just want to confirm the cause of death."

"Yeah," Max says quietly. He exhales through his teeth. "God. So sad."

"It's just . . ." My voice cracks. I flatten the emotion out of it. I feel drained, inside and out. An hour ago, I was wearing my persona like a second skin and it was all fun and games. Now it's chafing. A clump of mascara falls into my eye. My mouth feels dry, and my lips are chapped under the lipstick. I just want to become myself again, take a very long shower, and crawl into bed. "It's not supposed to happen like that."

We're silent for a moment.

"Did your friend say he talked to Ingrid?" I ask.

"Hasn't brought it up. I can ask," Max replies. "You want me to?"

"You'd do that for me?" I ask softly. It was a line Ingrid always used when she knew I would do what she asked but feigned uncertainty, anyway.

"Of course," he says.

"Thank you." I turn to the road; I can't look at him any longer or else he'll see the truth in my eyes, that all this is breaking me. "Just curious, you know?"

CHAPTER SIX

For the first time, I am actively seeking out Jackie Anh. She wasn't in today's AP Language class. Weird, because I swore I saw her pass through the lobby before the first bell rang. Did she get sick? Did she ditch? No, she would never. We've been paired as partners for this *Macbeth* essay assignment that's 20 percent of our grade because everybody else partnered up yesterday while Jackie and I were out.

She hasn't responded to my texts, either. I wander at lunchtime until I find the newspaper room, this small, closet-like space tucked next to the library. There she is, with her headphones on, furiously scrolling on her laptop. I open the door.

Jackie looks up.

"Where were you? You weren't in AP Lang today."

"Didn't feel like going." She crosses her arms. "What, did you miss me?"

Jackie cut class? Maybe no one is immune to senioritis after all. "A lot, actually." I match her sarcastic tone. "We're partners. For the *Macbeth* essay project."

"Cool." Jackie pauses. I stand there awkwardly. "You came here just to tell me that?"

I sit in the seat across from her. "Did the principal really yell at you for writing that article about Ingrid?"

At the mention of Ingrid, Jackie sets her jaw. "You tell me. You heard it all when you were eavesdropping."

"I wasn't *eavesdropping.* I was on my way to the school counselor because I'd lost my best friend in the world and I needed someone to talk to about it, okay?" I fiddle with the peeling corner of the table cover. "It was a beautiful article, Jackie," I say quietly.

Her expression finally softens. "Really?"

I nod. "And you know I'm not just saying that. I don't know what his problem was."

She sighs and slumps back in her chair. "It's the way I wrote it. The ending implied that there could be more to Ingrid's death than what we know." She rocks a little bit in her seat. "I don't think it was just an accident. I think someone else was involved."

My body feels like it's been plunged into ice. There it is—the shock, the confirmation. It's finally been said it out loud. That someone could be responsible for this. A long moment passes. "You think that, too."

Jackie darts forward, her eyes narrowing. "What makes *you* think that?"

"I just . . ." There is a strange prickling sensation running up my neck. "I don't know. No one just falls off a cliff, you know? I guess it does happen, but—"

"It wouldn't have been Ingrid."

"Yeah."

"She was at a St. Anthony's party that night. Dalton Burke's."

Hearing his name from Jackie's mouth is a jump scare. "You know the host?"

She rolls her eyes. "Ex–family friend. We went to preschool together. His mom's been so annoyingly pretentious ever since she got into Congress, though, so I don't really like them. But Ingrid went to his party." She clutches her head. "But then what? Where did she go after? The police keep insisting that she wandered around drunk and slipped and fell. But that's what I would expect. I always hear that you don't go to the police without a lawyer because they want to close a case as quick as possible."

"Who said that?"

"The true crime podcasts I listen to. My point is, something about that story doesn't feel right. And of course I say that and the school gets furious at me. Some bullshit about making sure to run the messaging by the administration. They just don't want people to think it was anything but an accident, because then it opens them up to scrutiny." Jackie straightens up. "Also, the superintendent of our school district is *very* close family friends with Dalton's mom. Representative Celia Burke. So maybe it's a reputation thing."

"Because they care about their reputations more than they care about someone who literally *died*." My words fall out brittle, angry.

Jackie crosses her arms. "I don't care what they say anymore. I'm going to figure this out."

"I want to help."

Jackie looks at me. "You're serious?"

"Ingrid was my best friend," I say. "And, I mean, you're the best investigative journalist around, right? And you have all your—podcasts."

"You're saying *podcasts* in a very derogatory tone."

I grit my teeth. "I also just called you the best journalist around, if you didn't notice that part."

Jackie preens. I already regret this. But I will endure for Ingrid. "You're right," Jackie says. "If anyone is going to figure this out, it's us. So." She pulls out a notebook. "What do we know?"

"Oh, we're going old-school."

"I don't want to put our sensitive case on the school Chromebooks and leave a digital trail. So yes, we're analog." Jackie flips to a new page. "The night of Dalton's party. Who was there? You were there, right? I think I saw you."

Jackie was there? I didn't even notice. "Yeah. Were *you*?"

"Yeah. Super briefly. Why do you look so surprised?"

"I just . . . didn't think you went to St. Anthony's parties." Or parties, period.

"Well, correct. I usually don't. But I got invited, and I came, got freaked out by the number of people, and then I got offered a mystery shot that I couldn't take because I drove there, and I thought of the future I would jeopardize if the cops came. So I left." She shrugs. "Did you guys come together?"

"Yeah. But then I lost track of her." I swallow. "I was—talking to a guy."

"Oh. Is it the cute guy you were making out with?"

Shit! How does Jackie know this? Which guy was it? She was there for all of three seconds. How does she always happen to be everywhere at once at the worst possible time? Maybe it's not all her—I've clearly been a little scattered as of late. I think of what Ingrid and I decided together on the beach when we came up with this scheme, seemingly lifetimes ago: *No one can know.* I hope Jackie says more. *Cute guy* doesn't narrow the field. "Yeah. Um, where'd you see . . . me?"

She gives me a funny look. "Upstairs? I was waiting to use the bathroom for a *very* long time." She pauses. "I think it was Aditya Kalra?"

Now I'm even more alarmed. I blurt out: "How do you know him?"

"I thought he looked familiar. Turns out, we'd met at the Stanford admitted students' meetup in San Diego. I'm quite good with faces."

I press my hand to my forehead, which is feeling hot. I can't even plausibly lie to get myself out of this. "Yeah, that was him."

"How'd you guys start dating? He's this tennis star, right?"

"Jackie. We're not here for you to interview me about my love life."

"So mysterious," Jackie huffs. "I thought we were just gossiping."

"When do we ever gossip about boys together? Do I know any of your boy drama?"

"Moot point. I don't have any."

"Right. Because you don't date."

"I don't date *boys*," Jackie says matter-of-factly. "Because I'm a lesbian."

"Oh—oh?" I'm caught off guard Jackie said that so casually. Did she just come out to me? What is going on today? "Is that, like, common knowledge?"

"Yes, but I haven't dated anyone at this school. Because I also don't date because it's a distraction from schoolwork." Jackie sits with herself for a moment and then turns to me. "Anyway. Let's talk about the night of the party. Ingrid was hanging out elsewhere. You didn't see her because you were with Aditya the whole night."

I wince at the implication that I ditched my friend to sleep with some guy. Even though I haven't actually slept with any of them. I promised them all it would happen on prom night, though I can't even fathom that happening, logistically or otherwise.

"I barely hung out with him. My mom wanted me to come home because she'd left the oven on, and so I asked Ingrid if she wanted to come home with me, but then she said she wanted to stay and that someone else would drive her home. And that was the last time I saw her." I check my phone. "That was around eleven thirty."

"And I came around eleven and left around eleven twenty," Jackie says.

"Did you see her?"

"No, there were too many people. We need to talk to people who stayed there after you left, then." Jackie goes to the next page in her book and writes out TIMELINE and underlines it. "Okay, so things we know right now. Ingrid arrives at the party at around nine thirty. Then . . . ?"

"I remember seeing her play stack cup with her theater friends." They all crowded in the corner of Dalton's kitchen. Huddled together, whispering, laughing, showing phone screens. Seeing this after what had happened on Ingrid's birthday was a deeper cut. Not that I wasn't already plenty occupied. It just seemed like a final blow, a confirmation we were growing apart. "Speaking of theater, I think she was talking to Cody that night." There were the Snap messages she received from him when we were walking up to Dalton's house. "He wasn't at the party, but they were texting."

"Cody Hill? That a cappella guy, right?"

"Yep. And the lead in the spring musical. Orpheus. He and Ingrid dated last year. Well, sort of. She really liked him, but he kind of just strung her along and would take her on all these dates but would never make things official. I didn't like him. I thought he was playing around with her."

"He's dating someone else now, right?" Jackie asks. "Val Becerra? Come to think of it, Ingrid *did* bring this up. I think she wasn't very happy about it."

"That's the thing. He is. But from what Ingrid was saying, it seemed like he and Val had been fighting lately. Ingrid was telling me that he sent her a playlist and also started sending her Snaps again." Ingrid told me all of her stuff about Cody because she couldn't really tell the theater group about him. Val was the co-lead of *Hadestown* and head of the girls' a cappella group. High school drama department royalty. I told her I didn't like Cody, but Ingrid didn't listen to me. She never did.

"So were Ingrid and Cody . . . ?"

"That's what I don't know. When I offered to drive her back, she said she was staying. When I texted her, she said someone would pick her up. I wonder if it's because she was waiting for him."

Jackie leans back, fidgeting with her rings. "Okay. I think he's definitely a suspect. And there's a potential motive, if they were . . . involved. And that makes sense with why she would lie about being at your place for a sleepover, because this is something she'd want to hide." She cracks her knuckles one by one and then picks at a corner of her thumbnail. "A lot of times in these types of cases, it's the ex. Murders are often committed by someone the vic—" She stops herself. "The person knows."

Ingrid was not the type of person who would let someone even cut her off in traffic. She would not take kindly to being referred to as a *victim*. "You must listen to a lot of these podcasts?"

"A lot. I think about this stuff more than I'd like to admit. True crime, unsolved mysteries. Cases that have gone cold."

"Okay, a little concerning. Is this what you do for fun?"

"This is not *all* I do." Jackie leans forward. "You've never, like, watched a true crime documentary before? Come across a video and then three minutes later you're sucked into a Wikipedia article?"

"That rarely happens. My feed is normal."

Jackie rolls her eyes. "Yes, we've established that you think I'm weird and neurotic. I like to figure things out, okay?"

The bell rings. We both jump.

Jackie looks down at her notebook. "Wait, wait, wait. Let's go over what we need to do."

"I'm in AP Psych with Cody next period. I can ask him."

"Newspaper's coming in next period. Liv Esposito from the theater crew is also a news writer. I'm going to ask her if she knows anything. Anyone else we can ask? Oh. What about Aditya? He stayed after you left, right? Maybe he can provide more information, too. Anything helps."

"I have a date with him this weekend. I can ask him more then."

"Great. We can debrief after." Jackie snaps her notebook shut. "Also, it goes without saying, but we need to be discreet about this because we know there's resistance from the school administration. If we need to come up with a code name for this, anything—"

What are we, the FBI?

"I'm not going to say anything," I promise her. "Also, I am vetoing any code name you try to come up with."

"Fine," Jackie says. People are coming in through the door. "And, um. Look. This is really hard. If you need someone to talk to about all of this . . . you can come to me, okay?"

For a moment, I'm flattened by the memory of Jackie's red-rimmed eyes meeting mine. Me crying in the counselor's office. My voice quavers as I say, "You too." And before I can be any more sincere, I grab my stuff and run down the hall to AP Psych.

Cody Hill wasn't in school the past two days. Why wasn't he here? Has he been sick? I briefly saw him at Ingrid's candlelight vigil, but by the time I was done giving my speech, he was gone. It wasn't just anyone's vigil—it was Ingrid's. Wouldn't he care more than to just show up for a few minutes?

He also seems weird today. Usually, he is laughing and joking around with the people next to him, but today, he's just silent. Staring at his computer screen. I watch him distractedly transposing "Uptown Girl" by Billy Joel on his computer as the teacher drones on about attribution theory.

When the bell rings, I pack up slowly. He puts his computer in his backpack and looks around. His blue eyes meet mine. I remember the smallest crush I had on him, back when we were freshmen and he was my seatmate for Chem, and we bonded over failing every other titration experiment. But then Ingrid got involved in musicals, and she started talking to him. She claimed him, they dated briefly, and I stifled my crush. It wasn't that serious.

I sidle up to him as he heads for the door. "Hey, Amelia," he says. "What's up?"

Make small talk. "Did you catch what Mr. Webster said at the end? Are our psych journals due this Friday or the next?"

"I honestly have no idea. I was so checked out."

"You okay? I haven't seen you in class the past few days."

"Yeah, I, uh . . . had a bad migraine." He turns the corner.

A migraine. Huh. "Wait. I wanted to ask you something else. Do you have a minute?"

Cody walks a little faster. Thankfully, I can take long strides to keep up. "I don't know, I have to be at Choir in—"

"The night Ingrid went to the party. What were you guys texting about?"

Cody stops in his tracks. He looks around, and then at me. "I wasn't talking to Ingrid."

Okay, lie. "You sent her a Snap. And I didn't drive her home because she said someone else was going to drive her home from the party. Was it *you*? Did you see her that night?"

Cody hustles us into an emptying stairwell. "Alright, listen. Ingrid and I weren't *talking*." What did she tell you?"

"You were sending her playlists. You were liking her Stories." Playlists and Stories she agonized over and tried to decode the meaning of.

"Well, yeah. As a—friend." He shifts his backpack strap. "She was just helping me with some stuff with Val. We were in kind of a rough place."

Now I am positive that the Snap was something of the explicit nature. "Right, because your ex-girlfriend gives you the best advice when you're in a fight with your current girlfriend. I wonder what Val would think of the logic."

"Jesus, don't tell Val, okay?" He combs back his long blond hair with his palm. "It wasn't anything."

Not anything? I hear Ingrid retort in my mind. *That's bullshit.* I'm glad he's flustered. It means I have leverage. There's a kernel of truth. Ingrid would press him, so I say, "*You* texted Ingrid."

"Fine, yeah." Cody spreads out his palms. "She texted me first. She wanted to hang out."

The bell rings, but neither of us moves. "So you did go to the St. Anthony's party that night."

"I didn't."

I narrow my eyes. "You weren't there?"

"Not at all. My boys and I—we were playing Jackbox games at Samuel's house."

"The *whole* night?"

Cody looks at me funny. "Yeah. Ever heard of a game night?"

"But it doesn't make sense. You were texting Ingrid a lot. And then you just ignored her?" I pause and cross my arms. "When did you go to your friend's house?"

"What do you want, a timeline?" Cody stiffens once he sees

I'm not in the least bit joking. "Fine. I went to Samuel's house around . . . nine, I think. I was there for hours. I got that Snap from Ingrid around . . ." He glances at the floor. "I think nine thirty? I remember because we were talking a little bit. *She* texted me through that night. At first we were just talking about, like, theater drama. Like, there's this freshman who's being kind of stuck-up. But then she told me she wanted to hang out. She told me she'd text me when to pick her up. I didn't really want to, because I knew there were theater people at the party and that they'd tell Val and we'd obviously get into a huge fight. But I waited for her to text me. She never did. I didn't think much of it. I thought, you know, she was just being drunk and saying stuff."

"So you didn't stop by the party on the way home or anything?"

"I didn't."

"When'd you get home?"

"Around one, I think." Cody lowers his voice. "I probably should have stopped by. I feel awful. I mean, at the time, I knew it wasn't right to pick up Ingrid, but I keep thinking, if I had . . . if I had been able to check in on her and drive her home safely, maybe she wouldn't have . . ." He slumps onto a stair and puts his head in his hands.

I sit next to him. For a second, I flash back to us as freshmen tablemates, laughing over the ridiculous lab-goggle marks on our foreheads. "It's not your fault."

We're silent for a few moments.

Finally, Cody stands. "I should probably get to Choir."

"Sorry I made you late."

"No, it's . . . just don't tell Val about all this, okay? Or anyone. This is just between us."

"Yeah. For sure."

I'm alone in the stairwell. I bite my thumbnail and text Jackie.

Me

It's not Cody he has an alibi.

Jackie

What's the alibi?

he was at his friend Samuel's house the whole night

Samuel Owusu? Wait I literally have AP gov with him next period, I can ask?

so we can independently verify this and see when the stories match up.

I pause.

OK but like, pls pls. be subtle bc Cody swore me to secrecy

I have no problem with subtlety

I roll my eyes. I find this very hard to believe. But what can I do but trust her?

Chapter Seven

Dalton lets me in. "Why do you smell like smoke?"

"Was just at a bonfire with my friends." I shrug my bag off and make sure I have cleared any sand off my body before I step foot in his pristine marble foyer. I kiss him. "You look cute with this apron."

Dalton and I were going to help bake something before his mom comes home tomorrow for her birthday weekend. But Aditya had texted me after school, asking me if I wanted to go to a bonfire with two of his best friends. They're so wholesome and fun and have been friends with Aditya forever, ever since kindergarten, and they're always so nice to me. I feel bad because lately I've been so exhausted and all I want to do is curl up under my blankets at home and listen to the playlists that Ingrid and I made together or scroll through pictures of the stupid shit we used to get up to. But I tell myself that I have to keep going on these dates for Ingrid. For what we planned.

"Oh? And who are these mysterious friends? Do I get to meet them someday?"

I shrug. "Only if we're serious."

"We *are* dating."

"But how do I know you're serious about me?"

I'm daring him to say it. *I love you.* How hard can it be? I know there's a reason. I know he speaks in flourishes, but at the end of the day, he doesn't know how to show affection. Hence his reputation of taking girls on dates for months, only to never make it official. Or confiding in someone at a party and sharing a kiss with them, only to never acknowledge them in public when he sees them again. Precisely what he did to Ingrid at summer debate camp. I've heard this story so many times. They competed against each other in a stuffy University of Michigan classroom for a practice debate. She won. He caught her after dinner the next day and they hung out for hours. Got ice cream together, talked about being from the same hometown and how cold it got in San Diego at night, how this soft Midwestern humidity felt so nice, marveled at the fact that their parents knew one another. At the end of the evening, while sitting under the willow tree near the dorms, he told her she was the smartest girl he knew and kissed her.

This is what I've learned: Most everyone has a first love that unravels them. Ingrid waited for something to happen after that magical night. But Dalton never asked her on a date, or mentioned the kiss, and Ingrid was too prideful to ask him how he felt about her. She was left trying to siphon meaning from his glances at her, or how close he sat next to her at lecture. We talked on the phone for hours that summer before sophomore year, unpacking his every action. I knew it stayed at the back of her mind. Of course it would all resurface the summer before senior year, when she saw him at the La Jolla Shores Beach Club.

Which is why, now, everything I take from him, any emotion he offers up, feels like some kind of victory for us.

But he's clearly giving nothing, so I change the subject.

"Okay." I stare at the ingredients tossed out on the kitchen counter. New packets of flour and sugar and milk open. Sliced fruit splayed on the cutting board. I'm peering over Dalton's shoulder, where he's stirring something clear that's bubbling viscously on the stove. "Is that *sugar*?"

"I'm trying to make caramel. I want to re-create this chocolate ganache toffee honeycomb cake that this chef made for her when we went to Paris." He pauses. "Oh. And I should check on the cake in the oven. It should be done."

He's trying to re-create something a French pastry chef made? We are reaching unprecedented levels of male confidence. "Have we . . . made caramel before?" This isn't something even Ingrid had attempted in *her* baking endeavors.

"Shouldn't be too hard, right? Just add the butter in when the sugar boils? You think I can use a meat thermometer for candy?"

I search for an errant fork, open the oven, and stick it in the cake. "It's not close to done. I think your oven's underheated."

Dalton exhales through clenched teeth.

Twenty minutes later and the cake is a disaster. Him having state-of-the-art ovens doesn't matter; he doesn't know how to use anything. The cakes are too flat and dense. The tops are dry and the insides are barely cooked. The caramel is burnt, so he stubbornly adds the baking soda to make the honeycomb, and it emerges a horrific, charred mass that looks like it's from a sci-fi movie. He swears softly and pokes at it.

Right then, the door opens. Dalton's dad strides in, phone clutched in hand, one earphone in. He casts us a bewildered look, which sharpens into an accusing stare at *me*. As if I was the one who looped his son into this. As *if.* I simply was a witness at the scene of the crime.

"What the hell is going on?"

"I wanted to make a cake for Mom's birthday weekend," Dalton says sheepishly.

Mr. Burke rolls his eyes and throws his hands up. "Just call Chef Mark and tell him what you want. We should have called him a week ago. And clean up. You know she'd hate to see a mess." He reinserts his earbud and starts chatting into the phone again.

Dalton tosses the saucepan with the goopy sugar abomination into the sink. He leans against the counter, his arms crossed, stewing silently. He's humiliated. Dalton hates when he can't get something right on the first try. Gently, I press a kiss to his back. He turns to me and opens his arms. I fold myself inside of them and run a finger along the side of his perfect, clenched jaw. "Hey," I say. "It's okay."

"I just wanted to do something special for her." Dalton shifts uncertainly.

Dalton has a complicated relationship with his mother, I know. She's barely home, and maybe that's the problem. He's always trying to please her, or rather, the phantom of her presence.

He chews at the corner of his nail. "Well." He sighs. "Let's clean up. I'm going to call Chef Mark to make her a birthday cake on forty-eight hours' notice."

I survey the ingredients spread out on the counter. Flour, butter, sugar. Chocolate chips in the corner. "Let's at least make something of this. Do you have brown sugar?"

"I think so. Why?"

"Let me do this. This treat's for us."

I grab another mixing bowl and a spatula. Preheat the oven again. I carefully measure out the flour. Sugar, brown sugar. Crack in an egg. This, I know. This is muscle memory. Ingrid and I have made this countless times. It's her prize recipe, her cure-all for a bad test score or an awful day—the essential for a holiday or a movie night. Already I can imagine the crispy outside, the gooey, chocolaty center. I melt the butter over the stove, stirring carefully until it browns and gives off this caramelized, nutty scent. I fold in the sugar. Combine and mix. For a moment I can almost hear her telling me to add in twice the amount of chocolate chips to make it double chocolate. I scoop the dough out onto the parchment paper. Put the pan in the oven and set a timer. I press another kiss to Dalton's cheek. "Okay. I'm going to try to get this caramel off my sweater. You can go call the chef to make your mom's cake."

I check that the coast is clear, and I head across the foyer. Jogging up the stairs, I turn on the faucet in the bathroom and then run to Dalton's room. I know what I'm looking for. I find his laptop, type the password I've seen him enter so many times. There's the Life360 app on his computer. Security camera footage. This was the reason I came over. I frantically scroll through the footage archives to the night of the party.

It's gone. The day of the party—from 9 p.m. on. It's all disappeared.

"Amy?" Dalton calls from downstairs.

I jolt up in his desk chair.

"The timer just went off. I think they're ready?"

"Yeah," I yell back. "Be right down." I hear the drone of his father on a call on the other side of the house. I stare at my own reflection in the darkened screen. He's deleted the security footage. Was this a precaution in case the police decide to investigate for evidence? Is Dalton trying to cover up the fact that he threw a party, or is he hiding something more?

I get home late with my stash of brown butter chocolate chip cookies. They're perfect, like they always are. I leave some out for my mom. She's left behind some winter melon soup and stir-fried veggies, congealed on the table, probably because she thinks I'll be hungry. She is always trying to give me too much food. I reheat some winter melon soup and pack up the rest into Tupperware for leftovers. I do the dishes. I turn the TV on and browse the channels, flipping to some show about antique finds. The apartment is dark and stuffy. I try to make it feel like home—I organize the couch pillows and light a candle, opening the windows so the cool breeze can come in. It soothes me. I go upstairs and switch on my laptop.

After eating a cooled cookie, I try unsuccessfully to log in to Ingrid's iCloud. If only I had access to her phone, I could get answers to everything. Her iCloud password is some combination of her childhood pets and a meaningful number. Her favorite number is seventeen. She always played soccer with that number. I try Loki17, after her childhood Australian shepherd. With an exclamation point. Neither works. I try the log-in for her school computer, the one I've seen her type in. Nothing works.

I lean back and sigh. I log in to my bank account. Three hundred dollars have come in from the Hermès scarf I resold. I've got almost eleven grand in there. I'd agreed with Ingrid to set aside some of it for donations to the nonprofits we discussed. The rest is going toward a potential college fund for my mom.

And then I do what I inevitably end up doing every few months: I look up my father's name. I scour the websites to see where he's at now. Records place him in Seattle or Phoenix. His name is all too common, though. Lin Wu. There are so many of them across the internet. I look for the age bracket: a man in his fifties. Still, it doesn't narrow down the results much. I poke around on Facebook, and then on LinkedIn, and on voting records. But I can't reach him. He's changed phone numbers. His email still works, but he doesn't respond to my messages. I've lost count of how many emails I've written him. I wonder if he opens them. I wonder if he has new social media accounts. If he's wiped every bit of his past life from the internet.

I sit back, fuming.

What is the point of trying to find him? I have dragged the same questions over and over through the recesses of my brain—will I find him someday? Will he return home? Who leaves with only a suitcase? I kept expecting him to come back for the rest of his dress shirts, for the Dodgers memorabilia he so carefully collected, so at last he could explain. Of course, deep down, I know the reasoning behind his choice. But just because I understand him doesn't mean I forgive him. Those are two different things to me.

My phone buzzes. Jackie's calling me. I pick up.

"Hey," she says. "So, Samuel and I talked."

I perch on my chair. It's almost a relief, hearing Jackie's voice. Better than my own thoughts. "What'd he say?"

"He's saying that Cody left just before midnight."

"Wait. Cody says he got home at one."

"Right. So I stalked Samuel's and Cody's addresses on the internet. They're twenty minutes from each other, tops. So what happened . . . to the other forty minutes?" She clears her throat. "He said he for sure didn't go to the party?"

"Yeah. He says he wasn't there at all. So either he took a really long time to get home or . . . or he's lying. Or maybe—maybe he and Ingrid met up elsewhere."

"Yeah. Because the timeline would match up, right? Ingrid disappeared around eleven thirty. If Samuel is right and Cody left before midnight, then they were both unaccounted for at the same time."

"Jackie," I say, tucking my knees into my chest. "What if it's him? I feel like there could be a clear motive. Maybe they got together and Ingrid threatened to say something to Val and then Cody lashed out?" Cody being violent. I can't even picture it.

"That's possible. I need to talk to his other friends who were at the game night to verify. But we're definitely keeping him as a suspect for now."

"Okay. Yeah. Let's do that."

"Let's look at our other leads. How was your date?"

I sit up. "*What?*" How did she know Dalton and I hung out?

"Weren't you going on a date? With Aditya?"

"Oh." I relax. "That's tomorrow."

"Are you prepared?"

"To play tennis?"

"*No*, I mean with your questions. Do you know what you're asking him? We can brainstorm a list if you want. Or if you want me to come, as backup, I could, like, meet him and—"

"You are *not* crashing my date." Imagine the questions Jackie would launch at him. Everything I've told him would fall apart within seconds. She stresses me out. I press the pads of my fingertips to my eyelids. "Text me any questions you think of and let's meet after. We can debrief."

Chapter Eight

"My dad wants to chat with you."

I freeze up for a second right as Aditya's serve streaks past me. As I chase the ball down, a million thoughts ricochet through my mind. This sounds serious. Is his dad going to press me on my start-up—has he realized that it's fake and now he wants his seed investment back? Is this about me trying to snoop on his work laptop the other day? I bounce the tennis ball as I step up to the serve line. "Oh? What for?"

"He was telling his VC buddies about your start-up. They were intrigued and wanted to hear more. A couple of them are coming to visit us next weekend, actually. My dad's going to do a grill night. You want to join?"

Oh. So this could actually be an opportunity. Before I can even register it, I blurt out, "Yeah, that sounds great."

Great. Now I need to conjure up a whole company. I wish I could body-swap with the real Eleanor Tsai. She, unlike Amy and Mia, isn't a figment of my and Ingrid's fevered imaginations—she actually is a senior who goes to Lakewood. When I applied for the tutoring gig for Aditya, I knew the competition was fierce and that his parents would do a background check. Eleanor Tsai, thankfully, had all of these recorded math and science competition wins and also had zero social media presence. She didn't even have any photos of her competition wins, just had them listed out on her *very* detailed LinkedIn. What a legend. I just basically became her, gave her a cute nickname, and added some personality. It's not like Aditya would ever cross paths with the real Ellie, anyway.

But it'll all be worth it. I still remember the absolute rush I got when Vineet Kalra wrote me a seed funding check for my start-up idea. I'd already been tutoring Aditya for some time. His grades were skyrocketing—half due to me actually being good at calculus and competent at teaching it, half due to me sharing my Ritalin with him. Or, sorry, Dalton's Ritalin that he shares with me because he's way overprescribed. (Call me charitable because I'm *all* about the redistribution of wealth.) I told Aditya to keep it a secret between us. It was good for him, and he was doing well. Win-win, right? His parents were over the moon, made me stay for dinner one night, where I just happened to ask Aditya's dad about start-up culture in the '90s and how he founded and patented the biotechnology mechanical tool that he ended up selling for millions, how he'd invested in all of these successful early seed companies before he ended up as the chief R&D officer for Bracken Pharmaceuticals. Just happened to mention how I was nursing a fledgling start-up idea. Three hours later, I had a check for five thousand dollars in my hands for Ellie Wu Tsai—a name I fudged around to spell Amelia Wu when I dropped it off at the bank. *That* high is hard to beat.

I would normally feel bad about swindling someone's dad out of this money. But due to his dad's billionaire status and the things he's done at Bracken, I don't feel guilty. Besides, I technically *could* found a start-up. So, yes, I will commit to this bit. Imagine another five grand. That's entrepreneurship, baby.

"Love fifteen." I toss up the ball for a serve, making sure to arch my back so that my low-cut sports tank rides down. But not even the sight of cleavage can distract a tennis prodigy. He smokes me. I hold my own for a few rallies, and I miraculously place a few shots that are in bounds. By the time the game is over, his hair is slicked back with sweat.

"That was good, baby. You made me run." He tilts his head and laughs. "You sure you haven't played a lot before? You seem like a natural."

"You're just a good coach. A few more tennis lessons and I'm coming for your spot on varsity."

"Maybe I should stop, then. Can't put my own career at risk."

I act hurt. "You're saying you don't want to hang out with me?"

"Oh, come on." Aditya pulls me into a hug over the net and kisses my forehead. I fall into his strong hug, feel his toned chest through his shirt. "You know I want to hang out with you literally all the time."

I nudge away. "I'm gross and sweaty. This ponytail makes me look like a Founding Father."

"That's too nice to the Founding Fathers. They don't deserve that."

"Any tips this time?"

"Yeah. Make sure to fully extend your arm to swing. Use the full length of the arm. And make sure you rotate with it. You're using too much wrist right now. That's going to give you an injury."

His fingers skim over my shoulders. I lean against him and

smile up at him through my heavily mascaraed lashes. "Sorry, show me again?"

"You're the worst student." He grins at me impishly. I press myself closer to him and his glance lingers over the neckline of my tight workout top. I know what looks good to him. My black top that acts like a push-up bra, the flouncy, flared skort that shows off my toned legs from running. I put on makeup, too, even though he thinks that this is all natural.

I love that there are no games with him. I can tell exactly what he's thinking. I lean in and without hesitation, he kisses me. Our rackets drop to the ground, and we're kissing over the net. My fingers skim down his arms, lift under his shirt to his abs. The tennis court gates screech and we jump apart. A pasty middle-aged married-looking couple are glaring at us. Aditya winks at me, wordlessly suggesting an even hotter car makeout later.

"One more game?" he asks.

We volley back and forth, and it feels good, lunging for the ball, my shoes skidding on the court. I remember my past life, summers doing drills and reaching place shots, long-limbed even then. God, I was so good. Good enough to win a summer camp tournament. I can lose myself in the game and think about what I could have grown up with in a parallel universe. Floor-to-ceiling libraries, summer camps for my whims, private tennis tutors, private lessons. Memberships at multiple tennis clubs. His family doesn't even live in La Jolla; they just have a membership at this tennis club because they like the view here. I think about all the girls I could have been and now can be. It's an exhilarating, screaming kind of freedom.

"You know, I actually really want to be a tennis coach,"

Aditya says when we finally sling our towels over our shoulders and lug the rackets out. "I just want to come back here and coach in La Jolla."

"Why don't you? You're good at it. It wouldn't be a bad life."

"My parents expect more than that."

"Oh."

"Like, I'm going to *Stanford*. I have to study, I don't know, business. I have to make something of myself. That pressure sucks." He pauses. "I think that's why my parents like you so much. You're the perfect kid in their eyes."

I press a kiss to his cheek. "You should do what makes you happy," I murmur. I hate that his parents are pitting me against him, but that's the only way I can stay in their good graces. "You're brilliant. You're so talented. Anyone can start a business. No one can play tennis like you do."

He brightens. "Really?"

Words of affirmation—his kryptonite. I find myself earnestly saying, "You're a marvel on the court. And you're so patient and good at coaching people. Really."

He hugs me to him. The car door's barely closed before his lips are on mine. I fold into his kiss and I think, *I'm so screwed.* I really, really like him. In the back of my head I'm running through the questions Jackie and I came up with together, but it's hard to keep focused in this moment. We break apart breathlessly. "Do you have water?" I look around. "Oh. Found it." I take the water from his cupholder and then go still.

There, at the bottom of the cupholder, is Ingrid's necklace.

My entire body locks up. I stare at the necklace in horror.

It's Ingrid's. It has to be. This is the heart charm I bought for her. The key charm I added this year. How did Ingrid's necklace end up here, in Aditya's car?

"Baby, what's wrong?" Aditya leans over, following my gaze. Then his wide eyes meet mine.

For a moment, neither of us says anything. It's Ingrid's necklace. I can't tell him it's Ingrid's. I'm not supposed to know. Can he tell I recognize it? Something darts across his expression—fear? Suspicion?

And then I do the only thing I can think of in the moment: I yank out the necklace and dangle it in front of him. "You're *cheating* on me?"

Aditya's eyes widen. "No—no! *Of course* not."

I screech, "What's some girl's necklace doing in your car? What are you doing with her?"

"No—there isn't another girl!" Aditya stammers. "This is just . . . a necklace I found next to my car the night of the party we were at. I thought it looked valuable, so I just kept it there."

It's possible, but an entirely suspicious and shitty excuse. I stare at Ingrid's necklace and try to figure out the reasoning. Was Aditya involved? In what world would Ingrid's necklace end up with him?

"There isn't anyone, Ellie. I mean it."

"You promise?"

"Swear."

I nod and try to keep tears from surging out.

"Hey. Baby. I'm for real. It's not like that."

Aditya thinks I'm just being the jealous girlfriend. Let him think that. I'm crying because I feel the memory of Ingrid possess me so forcefully that it brings me to tears. It's a relief to cry.

I bought her this necklace for her birthday. Aditya looks nervous. I turn and open the car door.

"Wait. Where are you going?"

"I need to go study with a friend. I'll call you later." I can't meet his eyes. I can't even see straight; everything is blurry with tears. The necklace is clutched tightly in my fist, and I can't let it go. I'm not leaving it in Aditya's car. I don't care if it comes off as erratic. I leave Aditya, slamming the door behind me, and run for my own car, locking myself in. I get out of there and just drive.

Jackie's waiting for me in the local library's study room. "Hey!" She stands and then her face falls as she watches me stumble in. "Oh no."

I slide the door closed behind me, with maybe a little too much force. I wordlessly drop Ingrid's necklace onto the table and slump into a chair. I'm still shaking. My phone is buzzing in my pocket with Aditya's calls and I reach back and silence it. "I'm so sorry. I had all these questions I was going to ask, and then I saw this and I just . . I had to get out of there."

"It's okay. What happened? You look awful."

"Thanks."

"I don't mean—like, you look very nice and put together, but you look pale and exhausted. Here. I got you this." She holds up a drink in a plastic cup. "Iced matcha latte from Sweet Pastime. I see you bring it to class all the time. I was picking up coffee, anyway."

For a moment, I don't say anything; I'm caught off guard by this small, errant act of kindness. Jackie is observant. I take a sip and it's heaven. I realize I forgot to drink water after playing two hours of tennis in the sun. And crying.

"Thank you," I mumble.

Jackie briefly nods. "So. What happened with Aditya?"

I nod to the necklace. "That's Ingrid's necklace."

Jackie's jaw drops. "You're sure?"

I give Jackie a withering look. How could I not be sure? I got this for her seventeenth birthday; the last normal birthday we celebrated together. Ingrid loved her birthdays; every year, February 17 was an occasion. I'd seen her through everything—laser tag in seventh grade. A big sleepover and spa night for her fifteenth. This one was special because it was her golden birthday, her seventeenth on the seventeenth. I'd be coming with her and her parents on a weekend trip up to Big Sur. *I* was chosen out of all of her friends. I'd just gotten a job, too, so I had a small savings collection building up in my bank account. I knew the gift I got for her had to be thoughtful. And I knew exactly what to get her. For years she'd looked longingly at the silver Tiffany's necklace with a hollow heart pendant at the mall. And so I depleted almost half of what I'd saved up through the years—all of that worth it when Ingrid opened it up with wordless joy, when she said, in a hushed whisper, *Oh*, and swept me into a hug, when she pulled away, her eyes shining with tears as she told me it was the best birthday present she'd ever get. How I felt a rush of happiness and relief when she broke out into a smile, told me that this was exactly what she'd wanted. I felt, then, this exquisite satisfaction, like it was a test I'd aced, like it was a confirmation that no one understood her more than I did.

We then piled into a car, and her parents took turns driving all the way up for nine hours, and we spent that perfect winter weekend hiking all around the cliffs and watching the sun set through the rock formations. And the whole next week at school, I'd glance over at her and see the necklace wink on her collarbone.

Now I cradle the pendants in my palm and hold the necklace out to Jackie. "I'm sure. It's this key charm. I had the number custom-engraved."

That was for her eighteenth birthday.

One of the things she'd always wanted to do was get was a tattoo when she turned eighteen. A small one, near her wrist—an iris for her grandmother, Iris Mitchell, who passed away when we were fourteen. When we planned it, she said she was scared of needles and asked me to come with her; I promised her I would hold her hand and distract her so it wouldn't hurt.

When her birthday came around this year, I knew I had to make it special. I asked her when she was booking the appointment and if she needed my help with that. Maybe we could get her tattoo and then we could go out to dinner afterward to celebrate her becoming an adult. I'd assembled a whole tattoo aftercare kit for her, with Advil and Aquaphor. But she seemed nonchalant. Said she was still considering the tattoo and that she might have changed her mind. I asked her where she wanted to go for dinner and she just shrugged. I ended up taking her to a fancy sushi restaurant where each course came out on tiny plates so we could savor the meal. I gave her a designer bag and this tiny key charm engraved with 858—our area code. "So you'll always have a bit of home." Ingrid smiled and slotted the key next to the heart charm on the necklace. We spent the rest of the drive home plotting the next move in our scheme.

Three days later, I saw the tattoo peeking out from under her long sleeve when we were passing each other to go to our classes. I pieced it together later, through posts and Stories. The night before, she'd had a whole separate dinner with her theater friends and gotten the tattoo with them beforehand. Without me. I saw it from several people's accounts, from several angles. Someone else was holding her hand while she got the tattoo. *I* had helped find the iris design. *I* was supposed to do it with her.

For days, I agonized over this. Had I done something? Had she hated my gift? Did she suddenly hate me? Why did she exclude me from her real birthday dinner? How could she go back on what we'd promised together? I observed her in class, sent her funny social media posts that she only laugh-reacted to, gave her every opportunity to explain herself. But she never mentioned a thing until *I* brought it up, days later.

Now Ingrid is dead. I can't begrudge her for what she did to me. I look at her necklace and I just feel a deep crush of sadness.

"This means Aditya is also a suspect," Jackie continues. "But what could the motive have been? He's dating *you*, right?"

"I don't know," I say hollowly. "He said he just picked it up at the party because it looked valuable. But that's a lie. I could just tell."

"And you believe him. You think nothing happened between him and Ingrid."

I say, softly, "You think he cheated on me with Ingrid."

Jackie runs her fingers through her cropped hair. "I wish

there just—I don't know. I wish there was just a record of this night. So we could see where everyone was and what they were doing. Footage or something."

Too late, I think to myself. "So, did you talk to more of Cody's friends?"

"Yeah. I talked to two more from their friend group. They said something different."

I lean forward. "Oh?"

"They said that Cody left at twelve thirty. Which lines up with his timeline now. You know what's stranger? Samuel texted me saying he got the time wrong. Without me asking about it."

"Do you think . . . ?"

"Who knows? Samuel did have the time wrong. But I also think that friend group talked. Maybe they all agreed on a story."

"They could all be covering up for Cody," I say.

"We're still keeping him as a suspect, for sure," Jackie says. "But we should consider other people. Aditya, for example. We just need more witnesses. I mean, let's go straight to the host, right? I could ask Dalton directly. Our moms used to know each other."

"No!" I blurt out. "I mean, I'll do it."

Jackie tilts her head.

"I volunteer for his mom," I lie, thinking quickly. "I'm going to be at an art gala with her tomorrow."

"An art gala?"

"Yeah, it's, like, this whole thing. Every year she has this local auction and fundraiser at the art museum in Balboa Park. I can try to poke around."

"Wow. You just happen to be in the right places all the time."

I smile weakly. "Helps our case, right?"

Chapter Nine

I'm in the art museum's bathroom, staring at the mirror. What does that necklace imply? The possibility that Aditya and Ingrid were seeing each other behind my back? Could Aditya do this to me? Could Ingrid? My eyes are welling up. I can't cry again, not when I've so carefully fixed my makeup. I'm wearing a burgundy dress. This was always Ingrid's color, so I've never worn it until now. Ingrid loved makeup and beauty and style, and so she always did makeovers on me. She said things with such certainty and conviction that they became truths to me. Red looked awful. Green looked better. God forbid I ever curl my sleek, straight hair, even though I desperately wanted to try. I let her put eye shadow on me a thousand times—once, when she revealed my reflection, I grimaced, thinking it looked garish, but she squealed in delight. I thought then that I must have been wrong, that I looked beautiful. Now I just retouch my mascara with the same kind of Maybelline stick Ingrid used and call it a day.

Eventually other people trickle into the bathroom and I leave. I emerge into a crowd of elderly San Diego retirees with very steely stares. This charity auction—part fundraiser, part birthday party—is the first time I'm meeting Dalton's mom, which is extraordinarily late, given how long we've been dating.

We met on Halloween. Became official just after New Year's. And yet, for the past four months, she's always been in DC or on some trip or another. The closest I've been to meeting her is over FaceTime.

There's a lot I need to do now. I need to impress Dalton's mom. Try to get Dalton alone for a moment and ask him the questions Jackie and I brainstormed. But what Jackie doesn't know is that Dalton might not be as helpful as she thinks. He claims to not know anything, and the security footage is gone. I used to think that immediately marked him as suspicious, but now I'm thinking that maybe he panicked. Tried to cover his ass by denying any involvement. Maybe his mom deleted the footage for him.

I try to quell my anxiety by admiring the beauty of this place. I haven't been back to Balboa Park, or this museum, in forever—I think the last time I went was as a kid—and I'm captivated by how the low lights filter through the lofty ceilings and seep into the cavernous room, draping over the ornate cabinets, the delicate sculptures, the cultural heirlooms that now serve as a backdrop to the paintings that local artists have created. I turn slowly, watching my satin slip dress ripple in this liquid light. I rearrange the aquamarine necklace Dalton gave me with my cowl neckline, which dips low on my chest. I text him frantically.

Me

where are you???

Dalton

Just finished my debate. Coming a little late.

From the corner of my eye, I see someone lugging a huge foam poster almost as tall as she is. I rush over and help her set the poster upright on the easel. "Thanks," she says, and darts off, typing something furiously on her phone. I adjust the poster board so it's perfectly centered and lean over to smooth out what looks like a scuff.

"Fifth Annual Emerging Artists Benefit Gala"

"You don't have to do that, you know."

I turn and I'm looking level into the eyes of Celia Burke.

I've stared at her congressional portrait and watched so many of her campaign videos and seen so many of her ads, and yet she's much more formidable standing in front of me, armored in a crisp white pantsuit with geometric patterns and perfectly blown-out, shoulder-length brown hair. She's tall like me. She's peering at me with the same deep-set green eyes Dalton has that I adore, but set with a thin smile that seems to threaten. In one sweep of those eyes, I know she's run a hundred tests on me in her mind, and I've likely failed most.

"Sorry," I manage to say. "I just wanted to help."

"That's so kind." She lightly touches my arm with her French-manicured fingertips. "Amy, is it? I am thrilled to finally meet you."

"Likewise." I nod quickly. I straighten up, partially out of fear and partially to prevent my neckline from dropping any lower so I don't flash a nip to a sitting member of our government. I do not have the chest to pull this dress off. "I'm so glad to celebrate your birthday with you," I say politely. "I hope it's been good so far?"

"My gift was my staffer booking me in back row coach on that six-hour flight from DC." She glares across the room at the frazzled girl with the clipboard I was helping out. Dalton's mom looks back at me and her features snap into a placid mask once again. "But my husband took me on a sunrise run this morning, and Dalton made me breakfast and cookies, so I am good as new. There is nothing like a beautiful day in La Jolla." She leans in. "And there's nothing better than to devote your birthday to something philanthropic."

"I agree."

"You go to the Day school, right? I was just asking one of our family friends if her daughter knew you, but she didn't."

I stiffen. Alarm bells start screeching in my head. "Oh, who?"

"Bailey Wright?"

"Oh, yes, I've definitely heard of her. I think we had Chem together. Weird she doesn't remember me." I shrug.

Dalton's mom narrows her eyes slightly. "Bailey is class president."

"So many people to keep track of, right?" I smile vaguely. "I don't blame her."

"Must be," Celia Burke says thoughtfully. "Dalton tells me you're going to Berkeley to study business, right? You must be a very accomplished young lady."

"Not as impressive as Yale." I hope my smile conveys, *I know you donated your way in.* "But Dalton's brilliant, so I'm not surprised."

I'm playing with fire, I know. But she's making me feel like I'm auditioning to be a Kennedy here, so I might as well have some fun. Her expression sours.

"Well. I'm glad he has you. He says you're very smart. That's more than I could say for the others."

I'm saved by her nervous staffer approaching. I ease out a breath, carefully step out of the way, and walk toward the center of the room. Finally, I can focus on finding Dalton—

"Mia?"

Of all people, Max's stepmom appears in front of me.

"Oh my god, Mia!" She folds me into a hug. "I didn't know you were coming to this!"

I feel like I've swallowed fire. My universes are colliding. No, collapsing. I glance around nervously, hoping Dalton's mom is out of earshot. The moment Dalton's mom sees me again, it's game over. "Hi Laur—I mean, Mrs. Bracken."

Max's stepmom grips me by the shoulders. "How did *you* end up here?"

Oh god. Now I need to pull off being two *separate people* at the same time.

I try to calm my breathing. I use the same excuse I did with Jackie. "I'm a local volunteer for the congresswoman, so I'm just helping out with this event." I straighten up, leaning into the bit. "How did you . . . ?"

Laurel Bracken knits her eyebrows together—or attempts to, anyway, since half her face is frozen. "I'm on the board of the local La Jolla Emerging Artists Foundation. Congresswoman Burke didn't tell you?" She looks around. "Bracken always hosts their holiday parties here, and I was walking the halls, and I was missing being a part of the art world, and I was thinking—what about the artists who are yet to be discovered? So I founded this."

Bracken Pharmaceuticals is one of the corporate sponsors. Now it all makes sense.

"We get to showcase all these amazing works and do it for a

good cause. As a constituent, it's *so* nice to be represented by someone who understands the value of art." She grips me by the arm. "Here. Let me introduce you to some people."

Now the dim lights of the gallery feel like an unwanted spotlight, and the ceiling seems to descend on me. This fun dress-up gala has now morphed into a minefield. I'm going to be trapped here for the next three hours. I nod and smile as Laurel introduces me to some of the patrons and donors. *Focus.* I can be Celia Burke's volunteer for now.

"Arts form the fabric of culture and society, as you know," I say. "It's so important to the congresswoman that we support the local artistic community and do everything we can to give back for a good cause."

Beside me, Laurel nods sagely.

Suddenly, I feel a hand at the small of my back. Someone murmurs into my hair, "Sorry, sorry. I'm here."

Dalton's deep, liquid, usually soothing voice now sends my entire body into panic. I whirl around. My mouth opens but no sound comes out. Max's stepmom is still beside me. Watching me. If she talks to Dalton, it's over. If she speaks a word before I can get one in, it's over. Dalton grins and leans toward me—for a kiss, maybe—and I do the only thing I can think of. My hands fly out and I push him away.

He stumbles back in shock. "What—?"

I wrest myself from Laurel's grip. "I need to talk to you. Come here." I turn to Laurel and the patrons. "I'm so sorry, excuse me."

I march down the gallery hall, Dalton following me. I need to put as much distance as possible between me and that gala. I run up the stairs and he keeps up.

"What's going on?" he asks.

I just quicken my pace. Finally, in a secluded, empty wing, I turn to face him.

"Amy, what the hell?" Dalton stands there in the middle of the gallery, arms crossed, breathing heavily, glaring at me. His shirt is slightly open at his collar and his hair crests in perfect gelled waves, falling into his eyes. He looks really, really hot. "What did I do?"

Dalton is an intensely private person. I used to dream of and desperately scheme for times like this, when he'd give me a look, or acknowledge me, even. Now I've rebuked his rare attempt at public affection and I need to give him a good reason. Or, just any reason. "Your mom doesn't like me."

"What?"

I lean forward. "You came late and left me alone with her and she was just, I don't know, grilling me!"

"Ames." Dalton pushes his hair back. "She kind of does that to everyone."

"I could just *feel* her judgment." I press my lips together and try my best to look upset. "I feel like she doesn't approve of me."

"Believe me. As an expert in disappointing her, I know what you mean." Dalton leans closer. "But that doesn't matter to me. *I* like you. And everyone knows it. I can go and talk to her right now."

"No, it's okay," I say. "I actually think it's better if we kept things low-key for this thing. It's too public." I look around and link my arm through his. "Can we just—stay here, for a moment? It's just . . . too overwhelming downstairs right now."

He laughs. "The Magrittes and Delaunays are a more

welcoming crowd than a bunch of jaded political donors pretending to fawn over paintings, I will give you that."

"How much do the paintings in that gala usually go for? A few thousand?"

"You'd be surprised," Dalton says gently. "The way my mom talks them up. We're going to watch a borderline senior scam unfold."

"It's *philanthropy*," I tease, echoing his mom's words.

"It's just so she knows who the most generous potential donors are to stay in touch with. Plus, she is fundraising for her campaign on the side."

A donor event disguised as philanthropy. Shit, Celia Burke. What a hustler.

"I prefer the company of these." He gestures to the art, turning to me. "And you."

I look up at him. He looks so sincere, so vulnerable, that I soften. I wrap my arms around him, under his suit jacket, and feel his warmth radiating through his dress shirt. The lean, toned back. He smells like salt and citrus. I trail my fingers where his dress shirt is untucked, sliding them under. At my touch he gasps quickly, and suddenly his expression changes, his eyes sparking with hunger. He pulls me in and he's kissing me in that patient, inquisitive way of his, sending shivers down my body. A warmth curls in the pit of my stomach and expands. One hand is on my bare back, pulling me to him, the other lacing through my long hair. He lowers his fingers, tracing them along my shoulder and following them with kisses, down, lower, to my neckline—

I gasp and point. "The security cameras."

"Don't worry about it," Dalton murmurs. "I know how they work. We're not in the line of sight."

As he kisses my cheek I tense up, remembering the deleted security camera footage from his home. What did he mean, *I know how they work*? "What, you have security cameras, too?"

He stiffens. "Yeah. I do."

"Really?" I pull away and feign surprise. "Wait, remember the case we were talking about a few days ago? Maybe that means you could pull up the tape? You know, to prove that nothing happened at your party?"

"It deletes every seven days. And it's been over a week," he says sharply. He glances around. "Why are we talking about this here?"

Another lie. I know the retention on his system is thirty days. But I can't press him further on this, and now he's suspicious. "Sorry," I whisper. "I just . . . I know you were nervous about everything around the party that night." He's impenetrable. My eyes fill with tears out of frustration, but I mask it as hurt. "Ugh. I wanted to help you. And now I've ruined the moment."

"Hey." Dalton reaches out and gently takes my arm. He pulls me into a hug. "I know you were trying to help."

I sniffle.

"You're so caring, you know that?" He presses a kiss to my shoulder. "That's why I love you."

Finally, there it is. He's said it so softly, it just barely echoes around the gallery.

"I—what?"

"You heard me."

I smile slowly. "I love you, too," I whisper in half disbelief, and pull him to me.

We kiss, this time ravenous and more frantic, until our lips are tender and bruised and we teeter on the precipice of public indecency. Then we lace our fingers together and sit on a bench and he tells me about the Delaunay painting in front of us, about the marriage of Robert and Sonia Delaunay and the Orphism art movement, and I ask him how on earth he can pull these facts and he tells me he saw their paintings in the Tate Modern in London a few years ago and never forgot about them. There could be a future version of us, as adults, dressed up at an art museum, maybe in New York somewhere, or Paris, or Florence, our fingers curled together, my head leaning on his shoulder. How can he hold so much in his mind? I'm dazzled—by how cerebral he is, his beauty, how carefully he lifts my hair and kisses my neck and sends warmth pouring through my limbs. We're making out in an art museum, which is as romantic as it gets. I tell him I love him again, but at the same time I'm distracted. The whole time, I sneak glances at the security cameras and think about the security camera footage. It's gone. He knows it's gone, and the deletion was deliberate.

At some point, Dalton's mom calls him and asks where he is. I tell him to go find her, that I'm okay being here for a bit.

"We'll keep this between us," I whisper to him as he leaves.

I know we're going to keep our distance from each other at the gala, that our fingertips might brush, but he'll be looking at me from across the room, turning our feverish kisses up here over in his head. I can play it cool with Max's stepmom. No one will suspect a thing. I hide out in the gallery for a little longer, still buzzing. I stare at the paintings with cheeks flushed, my fingertips against my swollen lips, feeling electric pulses arcing through my body.

I should go back to the gala. If anything, it'll be like with the boys at Dalton's party two weeks ago, but with their scarier parents. I need to keep Laurel Bracken far from Celia Burke and make sure they never interact. I take a deep breath, and head down the wing and down the stairs. I stop at the bathroom along the way and prepare for what's ahead. I wipe off any lipstick smears. I even check my phone. I see I have a string of texts from Jackie, checking in.

Jackie

How goes the information extraction?

Hello. Is there an update?

I sigh.

Me

Just as hard as I thought it would be.

The three dot bubbles immediately pop up.

Look who we resurrected from Do Not Disturb.

I roll my eyes.

Me

I'm focusing. Also, I can't tell you the updates when I'm literally in the process of getting updates.

Jackie

Do you want backup?

I just so happen to be in the area.

Now is my turn to send the question marks. What the fuck? No one's here with me in this bathroom but I stare at the mirror in fear, expecting her to just spawn over my shoulder—which, knowing her, I shouldn't count out.

no way you just happen to be near downtown san diego

We're literally forty minutes from home.

My dad dragged me to a padres game, so I am in fact downtown.

A picture appears. She is holding up a hot dog and looking very disgruntled.

I'm hiding out by the concessions.

I'm smiling in spite of myself.

I have never seen someone so upset to be at a ball game on a beautiful spring day

Jackie

Can't say I'm a fan of the sport. Anywhere is better than here

Me

Well, I'm hiding out in the bathroom from a bunch of judgmental elderly retirees, so. Not much better.

Trade you. At least you're actively sleuthing rn. Speaking of, what's going on?

Talked to Dalton. He was here

Great. What did he say

He doesn't have security camera footage :/ he says it auto-deletes after seven days.

But that's weird, right? I feel like usually security camera footage takes thirty days.

Really?

I pause. Jackie doesn't know I've been to Dalton's house. How would I know this information? I hastily text back.

that's what it is at my mom's hotel she works at?

Hmmm. He could have deliberately deleted footage. But he claims to know nothing, right?

Me

Yeah. But neither does Aditya. And I know something's up with him.

Jackie

Agree. still think Aditya's more of a suspect.

I have to get back. I'll let you know if I find anything else.

Please do. I'm incredibly bored. I will uber there if u need

I sigh. Having Jackie here would make things even more disastrous. I type, Don't. I'll come find you when I leave.

I steel myself in the mirror and tuck a strand of hair into my clip. Adaline Chen's earrings glimmer. I touch them for luck. I'm walking back toward the gala when I pass hushed voices in a hall.

"—just wish you went easier on her."

"I was very kind. I don't know what I could have said to upset her."

I hide behind a sandstone pillar. Oh *no*. Dalton's talking to his mom about me. He's usually so passive and noncommittal about everything. Why has he chosen today, of all days, to go to bat for me? To tell me he loves me? To shower affection on me?

"Whatever you said to her, it made her feel like you were pretty hard on her."

"I only asked her a few polite questions. I just find it strange that neither Danielle or Bailey know her, and they both go to the Day school." She sighs. "I don't know, Dalton. If we're being honest, something seems a little off about her."

I squeeze my eyes shut.

"Well, maybe it's just a big school, Mom. You don't have to sound like you're running a whole background check."

"What do you want me to do, Dalton? Should I give up on being a courteous host or trying to get to know your girlfriends? I might as well. I'm losing track of all your involvements. It seems like every time I'm home there's someone new."

"That's because you're never home."

When Dalton's mother answers again, her tone is frigid. "I have a job to do. Should I quit my job and leave all my constituents to fend for themselves?"

"Oh, it's always all about your constituents and not about your constituent who also happens to qualify as your son."

Wow, Dalton is *mad*.

"Well, I'm home right now, to spend time with *you*, and you're picking a fight with me on my birthday. I don't have time to deal with this on top of all the liability I have to deal with for you because of what happened. Do you know how hard I'm working, trying to keep that thing out of the news? Trying to make sure we have ourselves covered and tied up any loose ends? Let's just have a good family weekend, okay?"

Dalton's mom stalks off. Dalton fumes for a moment and then follows her. I stay frozen behind the pillar and then finally open my eyes. Dalton's mom knows the footage is gone. Maybe she deleted it herself and Dalton only knew after the fact. But his mom did mention the liability stuff she had to deal with . . .

because of Dalton. Was she covering something up for him? What did—or didn't—he do?

This feels like a lead to me. But there's no proof of anything, no record of the night now. I didn't even record this conversation—I should have and I'm kicking myself for it. Now Jackie and I can only go off my hearsay and eyewitness accounts.

When the coast is clear I finally walk into the gala again. I scan the crowd. Laurel holds court in a corner of the room, a glass of wine in her hand, effusively gesturing at a painting. Dalton's mom is on the other side. Okay. We can work with this.

Just then, one of the patrons approaches me. "Excuse me," she says. "You're a volunteer, right? Come help me here." She peers at her phone through glasses. "I want to donate to the campaign. They were saying it was possible to make a donation via Venmo?"

I look toward Dalton's mom, who's glaring at me now. An idea comes into my head. I turn back to the woman and smile at her brightly. I pull out my phone, pull up my own barcode, and quickly change my account name to Congresswoman Celia Burke. "Of course. Just scan this."

She pays and I strut away, my heels clicking on the floor in perfect harmony, like I was born to walk in them.

Chapter Ten

It's philanthropy, I tell myself when I duck into the bathroom and transfer nearly two grand from my Venmo account to my secret bank account. Ingrid would be so proud of me. Celia Burke won't even miss those campaign donations. Not with the corporate sponsorship of Bracken Pharmaceuticals. No wonder she gets reelected every cycle just so she can shuttle back and forth to DC to vote against lowering prescription medication prices, among her other crimes. If anything, I spared the kind elderly patrons of La Jolla from her scam. I'd kept up a precise orchestration, adjusting tablecloths and collecting donations in front of Laurel Bracken to keep up the appearance that I was a volunteer, while subtly herding her away from Dalton's mom at all times. When Laurel wasn't looking, I blew Dalton kisses after smiling sweetly at his mother to demonstrate that I was, in fact, a perfectly demure and unproblematic girlfriend. I have emerged victorious and unscathed—for now.

But it's time for the detective work.

I eventually weasel out of the gala with some excuse about all the homework I need to do and AP tests I need to study for. It is actually very true. I have my AP Comp Sci test, as well as Calc, and I just know I need to do three hours of practice tests tonight. It's a relief when I finally get to the parking lot.

Jackie really wasn't kidding about being close by. Petco Park, where the San Diego Padres play, is just a ten-minute drive from the museum. The last time I was here was sophomore year with Ingrid, at the Maggie Rogers concert. I still remember that perfect chill of the breeze, the whole stadium lighting up beneath us. The perfect night.

I compose myself when I spot Jackie in the parking lot. I drive over to her.

She opens the door, and I think her jaw drops. "Whoa."

"What?"

"You're . . ." She blinks a little. Is that a blush sweeping across her cheeks? "All dressed up. Shimmery." Jackie slides in and quickly averts her gaze. "I've never seen you like this before."

"That's because my preferred school uniform is a pair of plain jeans and various crewnecks," I say wearily. "It was a gala. I had to."

"No, I didn't mean that in a bad way. You look really nice."

I barely acknowledge her compliment. It's too earnest and makes me feel funny. "How's the game?"

"Still going. I don't even think we've made it past the seventh inning yet. Baseball games take forever."

"And you're at this game because . . . ?"

"My dad made me. Guilted me. He's still in there. I told him I was going to meet a friend and that I would meet him outside."

A strange, buried pain resurfaces. My dad used to take me to baseball games here every time the Dodgers were in town. Despite myself, I ask, "Everything okay with your dad?"

"He's just . . ." Jackie shakes her head. "We just got into an argument. I don't want to talk about it." She stares at her phone.

"Shoot. It's Sunday. We are supposed to submit a reflection for our *Macbeth* reading by tonight."

I forgot about our other group project. "I'm just going to skim the chapters later and write up something."

"You *skim* your readings? I can't believe this is who I'm going up against for valedictorian."

I shrug. "Maybe I'm just smarter."

"You are," she replies in a deadpan tone. This admission surprises me. "But I work harder. And if Stanford rescinds me because I can't read a book, that's going to be pathetic. I refuse to start slacking. Laziness is a slippery slope."

Never mind. The tenderness has dissipated. I can't wait to be free of her. "Anyway. Dalton. There's not much more I could figure out from him."

"As in, he doesn't know anything or he wasn't forthcoming?" Jackie chews on her lip. "Do you think that he's wary because he knows you were friends with Ingrid?"

Well, he doesn't *quite* know. "He says he doesn't know anything. Claims he didn't see her at his party."

"Which could be a lie," Jackie muses. "Otherwise, he would have handed over the security footage and cooperated with police. Although, maybe he wouldn't, because then there's evidence of underage drinking. Hm. Maybe he really isn't suspicious. Just trying to cover up the fact that he threw a party." She pauses and pulls out her phone. "Speaking of video, I got some. From Liv Esposito. One of the newspaper editors."

I lean forward. "*Really?* Can I see?"

It's a recording of a phone screen. The original video is

blurry. There are people in the foreground, playing some kind of drinking card game. But in the background . . .

"There's Ingrid," I whisper. She's moving around the kitchen counter. Leaning close and talking to two boys. One of the guys, the one in the checkered shirt, is whispering something in Ingrid's ear. The other is just standing off to the side, looking at her. He's wearing a bright blue polo shirt. I've seen that somewhere. The camera angle pitches, but he turns and I'm able to catch his face.

Max.

I gasp involuntarily.

Jackie watches me. "You know them?"

I lift my eyes to hers. I make a split-second decision. Aditya and Dalton, I let slip. But I especially can't talk about Max or that's going to reveal too much about what Ingrid and I had plotted. I want to take this on alone. So Max's friend *was* talking to Ingrid. Max might have been, too. "I'm not sure but . . . thought they looked familiar."

Jackie zooms in further. "I don't think they go to our school, or I would know them. But if we can find *them*, we can find out more. The video was taken at eleven forty-five. I think that's the last video that was taken of Ingrid at the party."

I need to talk to him. And who is the guy next to him? That was the friend Max mentioned on the drive home from the premiere, right?

A text comes in at the top of Jackie's phone screen. "Ugh. My dad says it's bottom of the eighth. I should go back. But next step, I'll try to figure out who these two boys are. And you should keep asking Aditya questions. I know he's your boyfriend and he's probably great, but . . ."

"He might also be hiding something," I say quietly. "I know."

Jackie purses her lips, I think in a sympathetic way. "We just have to consider everything. Anyway. Thanks for distracting me today."

"From what?"

She doesn't answer, just gets out and closes the door behind her.

I sit in my car for a bit. Finally, I reach into my bag and take out Ingrid's necklace. I take off the butterfly necklace from Dalton and fasten Ingrid's around my neck. The hollow heart charm is so cold, the metal feels like it's burning into my skin. I run my fingers up the chain. Put the charm in between my lips and swear I taste seawater. I miss her, so much that my body aches with it. I think of her lying on her floor, the necklace settled in the crook of her collarbone. Glimmering with the rise and fall of her chest. My cheeks warm thinking of the memory.

Right now we're just circling. What needs to happen is that I *need* to get into Ingrid's iCloud. That's going to give us sure answers. But what was her password? There's an infinite number of possible combinations. I grip my steering wheel in frustration and tear off my false eyelashes. I check my phone. I have two new texts from Ingrid's mom. We haven't talked much since the candlelight vigil; her mom, usually an immediate responder, has now taken days to respond to my texts checking in on them. I understand; she's been adrift in her own grief. But now she's invited me to dinner with them on Sunday night.

The next text is from Max, telling me to come hang out with

him and his family and take his yacht out for a spin on Thursday. I just stare at the text and then laugh in sheer disbelief. It's like he's read my mind. I needed to hang out with him, and now he's coming straight to me. I'll collect intel and bring it back to Jackie. How will I explain knowing the information if I just told Jackie I didn't recognize him? I'll figure that part out later.

Also, a yacht? What has my life become? I hear Ingrid in my mind, saying *Are you fucking kidding me? If you don't accept this date right this second, I'm going to be so mad at you.* I hear her all the time in my head now. And so, of course, I heart the message and say yes.

A yacht cruise on the open ocean is a lot less fun if you feel like you're going to hurl the entire time. The railing is cold beneath my cheek. Scratchy stiff linen cushions chafe my legs while I curse myself for forgetting to bring Dramamine. My toes are numb from the wind, and my nose is running. I am determined to enjoy this. I really shouldn't stare directly into the sun, but glancing at the horizon is the only thing that calms me, especially since the sunset looks so beautiful, like a yolk pouring into the horizon, seeping into the pink cottony clouds that sweep the deepening blues. I listen in on Max's conversation with his stepmom behind me.

"Come on. We can make this a fun grad trip. Think about it. All up and down the coast of Italy and Greece. We can even stop by Croatia."

"Yeah, but there's the trip that my mom invited me to."

"Well, sure. Start with us for a little bit and then go to the Alps. And maybe you can even come back after. Who knows? We might be in Corfu then." Laurel pauses and her voice goes up an octave. "Oh! Mia could come on this trip with us!"

At the mention of my name, I blink and turn with a placid smile, feigning ignorance. "Sorry, what? Is there a trip?"

"We're taking this thing for one last spin around the Mediterranean before we retire her," Laurel says, patting the cushion next to her. She's wearing a loose white top. The sunset brings out her beautiful blue eyes. "Just downsizing since Max is going away to college." She darts a glance to Max's dad, who's standing there, facing the ocean, texting on his phone. So far he hasn't contributed to the conversation at all. "She can join us, right, hon?" Peter Bracken's head turns imperceptibly. Laurel waves a hand at me and confirms, "Oh yeah. You can come." She looks at Max. "See, it could be such a romantic trip with Mia. You guys could have your daily excursions."

I know *downsizing* is an excuse. Laurel Bracken is not one to just get rid of a yacht. But of course they can't be sailing around on something named after her husband's ex-wife, can they? It's a pity. The *Therese* really is a solid vessel, even if she's doing crimes against my stomach right now. I pause a bit. I can't seem too overeager. I also am trying to figure out a time I can get Max alone so I can ask him about what he and his friend said to Ingrid. But I need to be patient. In a measured, passive voice, I say, "I'd love to come. Are you sailing this all the way there?"

"God, no." Peter Bracken finally joins our conversation—the first thing he's said to me this whole time. We've met briefly and interacted here and there, but he's always hurrying to his next thing, or in a meeting, or, frankly, in his own world and not interested in speaking to anyone. He now gives me a strange look, as if he expects me to have known about this. "It's getting cross-chartered. This is going on a shipping carrier that specializes in yachts. A superyacht transporter, if you will. It's a lot more cost-effective this way."

My head spins. Yachts on other yachts. I can't believe the word *cost-effective* was brought up in the vicinity of this conversation. I lean forward as if it's the most interesting thing I've heard all day. "How does that work?"

He brightens and explains the mechanics of yacht transportation. How the big shipping container waits in the deeper parts of the bay, filling up with just enough water so the yachts can glide right in. After all the yachts are secured, the water will start draining out, and the process is reversed. I can sense that Peter Bracken doesn't care for small talk but is animated by the things he likes. I thought he'd be scarier, but he really just seems like kind of an awkward guy. Laurel drifts away to help herself to the cheese platter. Max is out there, taking photos. Now's my chance.

"So," Max's dad says abruptly. "Your family is in the kitchen supply industry."

I stay put. "Yep. My grandfather grew up super poor in Surabaya, Indonesia. The war had ruined everything, pretty much. But he started this company in the '80s, manufacturing kitchenware. He was going door-to-door and hand-selling it on the streets. He worked until he was seventy years old and then my dad took it over."

"Remarkable," he says. "He worked hard so your family could have a good future."

"Oh, yes. He never let us forget how hard he works," I say softly. I tell this story with a lilt, a bit of my fake boarding school accent. "He used to gather me and my cousins at dinner and we'd play this game. By the end of the dinner, each of us had to come up with a business idea and pitch it to him."

"He was testing you," Max's dad says with a hint of a smile. He, too, is an immigrant. I am speaking his language. "Seeing who is fit to take over one day."

"I suppose he was. But that's exactly what I want to do." I level a smile at him confidently.

"Explains the NYU. Stern Business, right?"

"Exactly. How do you—"

He waves a hand. "Max mentioned it to me one time. I rarely forget the things people tell me. What's the name of your family company?"

"KioSana Supply Company."

His eyebrows knit together. "Think I've heard of that one. Well. You seem like a very driven young lady."

"She's involved in community causes, too," Laurel quips approvingly, taking a sip through a straw of her probiotic soda. "She volunteered at the gala I attended last weekend. For Congresswoman Celia Burke. That was fun, wasn't it?"

"Tons," I agree.

"She has a son your grade, doesn't she? The St. Anthony's kid who threw that party?"

I stiffen at the mention of anything related to Dalton and

freeze for a moment. Max's eyes flicker toward mine and Laurel watches me carefully. Her tone is strange. Her expression is curious. Did she piece things together when she saw Dalton come up to me at the benefit?

Max's dad saves me from wondering further. "I wish my son was so eager to take on the company. I had to beg him to intern for me last summer."

The Bracken Pharmaceuticals internship is notoriously hard to get. Ingrid got it last summer, but she's actually smart. She said that Max did nothing but lounge in his dad's office.

"I wish you were more supportive of my interests," Max grumbles.

"Well, I'm paying for your film school, aren't I? With your apartment and all your equipment? I'm allowed to express an opinion."

Max stares ahead, arms crossed. Suddenly he stands and storms off, slinging his camera equipment over his shoulder. I watch him go. His dad turns back to face the water. After a moment, Laurel unfolds her lean legs and pads over to Max's dad.

I go find Max on the other side of this impossibly large yacht, clinging on to the side for balance.

He's just standing there, camera trained on the horizon. I go up to him and wrap my arms around him. "I'm sorry," I murmur. "I didn't mean to ruin the vibe."

I feel the rumble of his laugh. "The vibe was fucked long before you got here. He never takes it seriously. I literally am presenting my short film at a festival in Hong Kong next weekend. I could be presenting at Sundance and he wouldn't care." He seethes. "For the record, he never thought I could take over his company. He never thought I was smart enough. It was always—"

"Your brother, I know." I pause. His older brother looms large in his life, even if I've never met him. Sebastian "Sebi" Bracken is currently in prison. Max found out he was sentenced the day he came to Dalton's party, and I'd spent half an hour comforting him while he cried on the balcony. They have a complicated relationship, I could tell. *Forbes* 30 Under 30, a genius investor, founder of his own company—until it was discovered that he was insider trading. I know it pains his family. His name is never brought up anymore. "How have things been since . . ."

"Since the sentencing?" Max turns away.

"Sorry. We don't have to talk about it."

"No, it's . . . I feel like a million things have happened since then." His one hand grips his camera and his other grips the railing tightly, his knuckles paling. "I hate him. I miss him. I feel bad for him. Prison seems awful." He looks sickly pale. He shakes his head. "I can't think about it."

"Hey. It's okay. He'll get parole. He'll get out of there sooner than you know."

"But things will never be the same."

That I have no answer to. I understand. There will never be a normal version of anything after what happened the night of Dalton's party.

We lie on the bow of the yacht for a long while, rocking side by side, watching the sunset.

I hear the click, and I know Max is taking photos. It's time to be his muse. I adjust my position subtly, so I'm arched toward the railing to create curves, the illusion of movement, pointing my toe out to accentuate my legs, tilting my face toward the vestiges of the ruby sun. I close my eyes and he kisses my cheek and slides his arms around me. There's no way to just casually segue into this conversation. Finally, I just say, "Remember when we were talking about Ingrid Mitchell the other day? The girl who . . ."

"Yeah." Max sits up. "You know what? I remember why she looked familiar. I worked with her last summer."

Took him a while to realize. I feign surprise. *"Oh."*

"I mean, we didn't really see each other or anything. Like, I think we were at one big intern lunch together. I didn't even recognize her at that party." He starts biting his thumbnail.

"Hm. So you didn't talk to her at all."

"Not really. She mostly hung out with my buddy Pat."

That lines up with the video.

"Do you know what they talked about?"

In the fading light I can't be sure of his expression. Does he look pensive or nervous? "Honestly, I'm not too sure. I think they were talking about this musician they both really liked. Apparently they kissed in the wine cellar later. That's all I heard from him."

I've seen him in pictures with Max. He has curly shoulder-length strawberry blond hair that he ties half up. Ingrid kissed him? After she texted Cody to pick her up? There are so many things that I didn't know she was up to that night.

"And then what? What happened with Pat?"

"Nothing really happened beyond that. He said Ingrid ran out on him."

"Did you see him for the rest of the party?"

"Yeah. I mean, he wandered off for an hour. Told me he found some other girl."

Right when Ingrid disappeared. "You believe that?" The words fly out before I can stop myself.

Max stiffens. "Of course I believe my friend. What are you saying?"

Too close, too close. I need to remain calm. What *am* I saying? That I believe Max's friend had something to do with Ingrid's death? "They say she got too drunk and stumbled off a cliff."

"Did *you* talk to her?"

Max sounds suspicious. Did he see our conversation upstairs? He couldn't have. He would have brought it up way sooner. Besides, we didn't say much. Or rather, Ingrid didn't say much. I'd cornered her and asked her, point-blank, what was wrong between us. She just avoided eye contact, took a sip of her drink, and went to find her other friends. "No. She never talked to me."

The boat rocks a little, and my concentration is overcome by another wave of nausea. I lean over, putting my head between my knees. Max rubs my back and steadies me. I take deep gulps of the salty ocean air and then lean back, settling into his strong arms. The nausea subsides. Tracing patterns on the back of his hand, I turn my focus to the film he's presenting in Hong Kong next weekend. I fawn and ask him questions, per my girlfriend duties. We pull into the bay. Before I step off the yacht, Laurel pulls me in tight and I can smell her expensive orange blossom perfume, and she tells me I must come with them on the Mediterranean trip this summer. I try to picture myself lounging on this very yacht in the Mediterranean, three months from now, surrounded by turquoise blue seas and cresting mountains. Swimming to perfect golden beaches. I'd made a promise to myself to break up with all of them before prom. I'd originally started doing this because Ingrid and I were in on it together for revenge, because I wanted to make a little money on the side to help with tuition and support my mom's college dreams, too. But when else will I ever get to go on a trip like this? Now that I've claimed this life, how could I ever let it go?

Chapter Eleven

Jackie and I puzzle over the timeline in AP Lang the next day. All the groups get to spread out, so we go into the hallway to work. Instead of collaborating on this partner paper, we slot all our information from the night of the party into a color-coded timeline: I drove Ingrid to the party. She hung out with her theater friends. She texted Cody but he didn't come pick her up. Ingrid and I had our conversation. She talked to Max's friend Pat. At some point, she and Pat snuck to the wine cellar and kissed. She then left Pat in the wine cellar. And then she went—where? Outside? Did she see someone else? Did she go for a walk in the darkness only to lose her balance and fall?

"Any other clues?" I press. "Anyone else she could have talked to, or anyone who's offered any information?"

"No," Jackie answers flatly, scrolling on her phone.

"Are you looking up Patrick Hayden's freshman-year basketball stats on Hudl?"

Jackie looks up. "Anything could be helpful, Amelia."

I have serious doubts about this one. "You think he could have done it?"

"You're the one who volunteered with his friend over the summer." That's the excuse—that I worked with Max Bracken's friend volunteering for Celia Burke, and so I'd met Max a few times. "Why don't you ask him?" Jackie sits up. "Or better yet, why don't you send me in?"

"I *will* ask. We can come up with questions together."

"Why are you always so secretive?" Jackie frowns. "You know we can work together on asking people, right?"

"Yeah. You have your people you ask. I have my people. We're still tracking Cody as a potential suspect, right? Maybe you could follow up with his friends."

We finally agree to call it for the day and then make plans to meet up this weekend. Jackie says she's busy Saturday with a bunch of stuff, and also, she and her mom have their weekly movie night, but maybe I can come over to her house on Sunday morning. I do find it endearing that she watches movies with her mom every week. Maybe my mom and I should have something like that. Mostly my mom puts on TV shows in the living room, and I linger if I'm interested. I wonder why Jackie's dad isn't included in the movie nights—are they divorced, maybe? That really isn't my business, but still, I wonder.

The timing works for me, anyway. Saturday is Dalton's debate tournament, and throughout the week I plan an increasingly elaborate beachside picnic for afterward.

That Saturday morning, I buy his favorite turkey sandwiches from this artisanal bread place. Later, I buy organic grapes from the farmers market. I get those table crackers that taste like stale wrapping paper. I get two different kinds of cheeses. I get the dark chocolate–covered pretzels. I've tucked little notes in everywhere.

I know he loves getting surprised, so I show up early. The high school he's competing at looks surprisingly like mine.

People are sitting cross-legged in their fancy suit outfits, hunched over computers. Passing a room where people are rattling off arguments at an unintelligible speed, I find my way to the room where Dalton is competing. I slip inside.

He's just stood up to cross-examine his opponent when his eyes find mine. It's immediate, the way his face lights up. I smile back at him, hold up the chocolate-covered pretzels, and mouth *You got this*, though he doesn't need my luck. He's competing in a Lincoln-Douglas debate, so it's one-on-one. I don't even understand the first thing he's saying—something about values and impact—and it's all far too fast for me. But what is clear, even to me, is that he seems far more charismatic and logical than his opponent.

When the round is over and the judge is deliberating, he heads straight toward me. I grin up at him and wordlessly offer the bag of pretzels. He tilts his head toward the door and I follow him out. He takes the bag and gives me a sly smile. "You came to this place of your own free will?"

"What?" I gesture around me at the water fountains, whose lights are blinking yellow. "Isn't this the place to be on a weekend?" I fish pretzels out of his bag. "Heard there was a hot star debater here. Had to come see for myself."

"Well, you're about to see me lose."

"But you sounded great."

"I dropped an argument. It's a technicality. I know I'm screwed." He tosses up a pretzel and catches it in his mouth. He looks incredibly good right now, in the slacks and loose-collared shirt that just exposes a bit of his throat, showing off the silver chain that I bought for him. A few people pass by.

"What's up, DB?" someone says.

He nods at them. "Just people from debate camp," he explains to me after they pass. He guides me with his hand to the small of my back, keeps it there, and my breathing quickens. I feel warm inside. Dalton isn't big on PDA at all—he's much more into hidden kisses and small gestures—but he's been leaning more into being affectionate these days.

"Let's get back in there," he says. "This place is built like a labyrinth."

"I'm pretty sure the school is a circle."

"That's what they want you to think. Other way, let's go." He playfully nudges me away from taking a wrong turn and slings his arm around me, cupping my jaw and giving me a kiss.

"Dalton?"

Standing in front of us, looking like a 1950s secretary on her way to a funeral in her black skirt suit speech uniform, is none other than Jackie Anh. I immediately drop Dalton's hand. This has got to be some kind of insane cosmic joke. She's on the speech and debate team? When will the list of extracurriculars end?

Jackie looks over at me. She points a finger at him, and then points it back at me, and then at him again. "Wait. Hold on. Amelia? What—are you guys—?"

It's like a spell has been broken. Now that she has said my actual name, anything can happen, and I'm just frozen.

She saw us *kiss*.

The door opens. "Dalton? A decision has been made."

I tug on Jackie's arm. "Jackie and I are going to get some water. We'll come find you when you're done."

I drag a protesting Jackie behind me. All I can think of in this moment is putting space between me and Dalton. We go down a labyrinthine set of hallways, and then another, and finally Jackie yanks her arm out of my grip and says sharply, "Where are we *going*?"

"Getting water," I say automatically. *Delay, stall, explain, do whatever you can.*

"What are you doing here with Dalton Burke? I thought you worked for his mom."

"What do you mean? I do. And then we became friends."

"That was *not* friend behavior I just witnessed," Jackie accuses, trailing me. "You guys kissed! You're cheating on Aditya?"

"I'm not!"

Dalton was right—this place is a maze. I finally give up on going somewhere and whirl around to face her. The bright fluorescent ceiling lights bear down, making me feel disoriented. I stare at the endless hallway of paint-chipped blue lockers and feel like they're closing in on me. I start rambling.

"*He* kissed me, okay?" I tell her. "I didn't see it coming. I thought we were just friends because I worked on his mom's campaign, and then he asked me if I could come to this speech and debate tournament to support him. And, you know, I thought I was just doing it to be a friend to him this entire time, and then he just *kisses* me out of nowhere."

Jackie just blinks. Finally, this appeases her. "So you—"

"I promise there's nothing between me and Dalton," I say. "I'm dating Aditya."

"You're dating *who*?"

I turn. Dalton is standing there, his mouth agape.

My own lips part, but nothing comes out. Everything seems to crumble around me and collapse into this one moment: beyond explanation, beyond reasoning, beyond the point of return. When my body jolts back into motion, I do the thing I have never ever done.

I turn and I run.

Part Two

The Reveal

Chapter Twelve

I flee the high school. I drive—first toward home, but then I take the exit that leads to Moonlight Beach. It's a strangely cloudy day and windy out, so there are not that many people here. I lug my picnic basket to an isolated rock and devour the sandwiches I brought for Dalton and me. I stuff myself with chocolate pretzels and inhale two kinds of cheeses until my stomach hurts, but still I keep eating numbly as I look out at the gray sea. Everything Ingrid and I planned is now over. Ruined by Jackie. Should I have stayed at the tournament? Tried to explain myself out of the situation? There was no way. Jackie had seen too much. I look at my phone. It's silent but I just know that Jackie and Dalton are talking right now. Any moment now, I will get a flood of texts from them both, asking me to explain. The wind at the beach is fierce and my eyes are smarting. I turn off my notifications. I throw the rest of the picnic basket away—probably seventy dollars' worth of food—and, finally, I drive home.

My mom's inside, sorting through paperwork at the kitchen table. She hears me come in.

"Look! The hotel company is hosting scholarships for the kids of their employees. Maybe you should apply?" She glances up at me and her smile drops. "Baobei? What is going on?"

What do I even tell my mom? I'm not crying hard, but tears

keep welling up in my eyes. "M-my tutoring," I finally manage. "One of my . . . students quit."

It's a pathetic excuse.

"Why?" Mom stands. "Were you not a good enough teacher? What happened? Tell me everything and let's figure it out."

I let my shoulders rise and drop. "I don't know." I'm exhausted. I know my mom's trying to help, but I can't take any more interrogating.

"This is not something to cry about," my mom says firmly. "You can get other students! Didn't I recommend you one of my coworkers' kids the other day?"

"I know."

"Do you want me to call her?"

"No!" I blurt. "I can—just let me figure this out myself."

"I know you're hardworking, Amelia," she says. "But I can help you if you need. Just tell me. Is it just about your student? Or is it something else?"

For a moment, I consider telling her everything. About the relationships, the false identities, and what I did. But I can't even imagine how she would react. My mother, who has never taken a penny from anyone, who has never told a lie. I think it would actually break her. I think of the promise I made to myself years ago—that I would never let my mom worry about anything related to me.

"I just don't feel well right now," I mumble. "I think with Ingrid . . . everything's been hard lately."

She nods and pulls me into a hug. "Go rest, then," she says. "I'm going to make some goji berry tea for you. We will figure this out."

We will figure this out. Mom always said this after Dad left. She said it to me but mostly to herself, repeating it as a prayer, as reassurance, as something she willed into certainty. She was determined to raise me, to make sure I was taken care of, to make sure I got into college. When I got my acceptance letter from Berkeley last month, she burst into tears and said, *We figured it out.* We really did. That's what we did as a family.

I go upstairs and crawl into bed. I'm not sure if I'll even be able to fall asleep at some point. By the time I emerge out of my fugue state, it's almost dark out. I go downstairs. Mom has gone to work. The goji berry tea she made me is cold and oversaturated, but I sip it anyway. Was there ever a chance I could have saved it all and talked my way through it? I could have told Dalton that Jackie was unhinged; I mean, that's not even a lie. For all he knows, she could be making all this up.

Come on, Ingrid says in my head. *After everything we worked for?*

I lean against the counter and drink my tea. I know it's a long shot, but I grab my phone. It's still on Do Not Disturb. I don't even want to think about how many texts from Jackie are behind that. Instead, I dial Dalton directly. It rings through to voicemail. I grip my phone tightly in my hands. *Come on.* I dial again.

There's a click as he picks up. For a moment, I'm shocked I made it through.

"Hey," I say breathlessly from sheer relief. But there's just silence on the other end. *Think.* I need to make up something on the spot. As long as we're talking, I can save this. "Sorry for just leaving like that earlier. I just got so mad at Jackie for mixing me up with another girl who went to your party and I just—" My voice rises. "I just shut down."

There's a silence. When he speaks, his voice is careful, measured. "So you . . . you weren't kissing another guy at my party?"

"Of course not. I was with you that night. Remember? I mean—" I soften my voice, make it syrupy and thick with emotion. "I love you. I would never."

There is another long silence.

"You have this fascinating mind," Dalton says finally. "I remember when we first met, I was always just trying to figure out what you were thinking—really, truly thinking. It drove me insane, and I also loved that about you. You were so—*beautiful* and your mind was this great puzzle, and yet at the same time I had never met anyone else who just understood me so immediately."

I ease my grip on my phone.

"So, tell me, Amelia Wu. How did this brilliant mind come up with the persona of Amy Fang?"

A small involuntary gasp escapes my lips.

"Was any of it real? The stories you told me about yourself? Did your parents die in a plane crash? Were you ever at boarding school? Did you really have to come up with such a ridiculous backstory?"

I'm numb. I'm not physically with Dalton, yet I feel pinned down by his questions. It is really, truly over. I laugh weakly, and in my shock, I answer honestly. "That was the only way to get your attention."

"Well, you got it, you freak."

I recoil. I'd expected him to raise his voice, but his calm demeanor feels even scarier.

"We're over. Don't ever talk to me again."

The call ends.

I try to text him, but I get a notification that the texts weren't delivered. He's blocked me. I gnaw at the edges of my cuticles until I feel a slice of pain. I can't even look at the texts that Jackie has sent. Has she continued her rampage and informed Aditya? Does she even know how to reach him? They've only crossed paths once at a Stanford event, right? She's the nosiest person on the planet; leave it to her to find out.

When a Snap comes in from Aditya, unprompted, I jump, fearing the worst. But he's sent a picture of himself, snuggling with the plushie that I won for him on our date at Dave & Buster's.

gn bbgirl

Relief pours over me. I clutch the phone to my chest. He's still sending me his daily good-night Snap. We're going to be okay. Maybe Dalton has broken things off, but the others don't have to know. It's not like they're all friends, anyway. I do my makeup quickly and transform from sad sack in bed to hot girlfriend and send a Snap back. I'm going to see him after tennis practice tomorrow, and we're getting lunch together, and then I'll think of what to say to Jackie. All is not lost.

As I sink back into bed, part of me misses Dalton. Only he could match me. Aditya just seems to agree with everything, and I don't share any of my inner thoughts with Max so I can stay the chill, unbothered girl he fell in love with. But Dalton can spin conversations out of nothing. He has a way about him that makes you confide in him. Maybe that's why Ingrid liked him. I think about us locking eyes at his Halloween party and then a month later at the bookstore, the games of emotional detachment and closeness we played, the thrill in the way we chased each other—no texts for days and then an article link and ten texts in a row. Radio silence and then a three-hour call that stretched to midnight. Us at the museum, fingers entwined, my head on his bony shoulder. But now he's won because of Jackie and her big mouth. And I'll never get to finish what I promised to Ingrid.

Ingrid. Dalton was my key to the security camera footage. I just know something is up with that; whether he was directly or indirectly involved, talking to him was my only way of finding out. And now I will never get to.

Jackie never texts me, so I assume we're not hanging out on Sunday morning. Instead I start getting ready for my lunch date with Aditya three hours beforehand. I lay on false lashes, coat them with layers of mascara. I put on yoga pants that show off my legs (and, to be honest, my butt) and a loose, cropped, shredded sweater that drapes over my shoulders and flashes my toned stomach when I stretch. Between my habit of running all the time to clear my mind and my tennis sessions with Aditya, I've actually gotten really into shape. I pick up his favorite flavored caffeine soda waters at the grocery store and drive up the coast around ten thirty in the morning to his high school. As I wave hi to some of his teammates, I tilt my head a little and smile. Aditya is one of the last people to pack up. He's talking to the coach. He's nodding at something. And then he slings his bag over his shoulder, turns, and sees me.

He just stares, not making any move to come toward me. When he does, it's a slow gait. His shoulders are slumped. Did something upset him at tennis practice? I know his coach is sometimes hard on him because he's the star player of the team, and Aditya is sensitive at his core.

Finally, he stops in front of me.

"Hi," I say sweetly, holding up one of the Celsius drinks.

He doesn't take it and instead looks me dead in the eye. "Are you cheating on me?"

I drop my arm and lurch back. "What?"

"Yes or no? Have you been cheating on me with a guy from St. Anthony's?" Aditya crosses his arms. "I think I know the answer, but I'd love to hear it from you."

He knows about Dalton. I burst out, "No! How did you—"

"This guy named Dalton says some girl was catfishing him and dating him with a whole fake identity. He sent over pictures, and I just knew it was you." He drops his tennis bag on the ground. "I mean, who the hell *are* you, Ellie? Are you even Ellie? Who am I talking to?" He turns away and yanks off his headband.

There's just simply no way to come back from this. But I can't break up with him. Beyond anything else, it'll blow my cover to look into Ingrid's death. To find out if he was involved. The *necklace*. I need to ask about the necklace!

"I *am* Ellie," I plead, and the tears in my eyes are real. "Come on. You can literally look me up on the internet."

"I was going to prompose to you today, you know," Aditya says dully. "And now I'm never going to trust anyone I date again."

He's so beautiful standing there, with the sun beaming down on his smooth cheekbones, those deep brown eyes I love, his curly hair, even the ears that stick out a little bit. Even in his heartbreak he is earnest. The hurt is written plainly on his face.

"I introduced you to *everyone* in my life," he continues. "My parents. My friends. I even told my sister about you. She was so excited to meet you at graduation. And the entire time, you never brought me over to your family or around any of your friends." He laughs. "I should have known then. For all I know, you don't have any friends. You're just a friendless psycho and a pathological liar."

A friendless psycho. That is the thing that finally knocks the wind out of me. I stagger back, tears rolling down my cheeks at the cruelty of that accusation. But Aditya—gentle, sweet Aditya—doesn't move forward, or comfort me, or offer me a hug. He just coldly pushes past me, snatching the drink out of my hand. "And I'm going to have to find a new prom date."

It hurts so much because it's true. Beyond Ingrid, I had no one. Maybe I am finally admitting to myself that going on dates was a kind of reprieve, a distraction to salvage me from the depths of my grief. How pathetic it was that it took me becoming fake people to escape being crushed by this loneliness. And now it's only a matter of time before gossip flies around, and Max finds out, and I will really, truly be alone. And probably canceled on the internet five times over.

Part of me did love them. Amy Fang and Ellie Tsai weren't separate entities; they were all me. I was having fun but I didn't mean to be callous about it. Even in spite of everything—their staggering, grotesque levels of wealth and privilege—there was something endearing about them to me. It *does* sting.

But the worst thing is that I failed myself and Ingrid. I remember sitting on Ingrid's carpet, coming up with this plan. Returning from each date and debriefing, giggling, one step closer to it all. We had a mission. And after Ingrid's death, I needed to stay close to the boys to figure out what really happened.

Now I'm cut off from them and alone in all of this.

I think of Aditya calling me a friendless psycho over and over again, and, defeated, I sink into my car's front seat and just cry.

Chapter Thirteen

I want to stay in bed and wallow all day, but I need to pull it together because I'm supposed to go to Ingrid's house for Sunday dinner tonight with her parents.

When I think of the best times with Ingrid's family, I always think of New Year's Eve. They regularly took me in that night because my mom had to work overtime at the hotel. Ingrid's dad would put shrimp on the grill. Her mom would make a lasagna and perfect, crispy, oven-baked brussels sprouts. After dinner, Ingrid and I would bake her brown butter chocolate chip cookies in the kitchen and eat them on the couch, her huge couch that you could sink all the way into. Her parents would sneak us some champagne. And that was how we always rang in the New Year; cozy, piled on the couch, watching the ball drop in New York at 9 p.m. our time with their goldendoodle puppy, Peanut, curled up next to me.

Now Peanut nips at my knee while I'm eating pizza slices in their kitchen. It's good pizza—it's from Isola—but the state of their kitchen and the take-out boxes piled high tells me that they haven't cooked, not for a long time. Ingrid's mom moves around the kitchen aimlessly, filling water glasses that we've barely taken sips out of, passing me another napkin every few minutes.

The dog pounces on my knee again, reaching for my pepperoni slice. I lift it out of the way.

"Peanut!" Ingrid's dad scolds.

"How is school these days, Amelia?" her mom asks me.

I sigh. "It's fine."

I'm dreading going to school tomorrow. I know my grades are slipping, and that I'm likely going to lose the valedictorian spot to Jackie. I worked so hard for four years to keep that from her. But I think it's beyond saving now. I'm definitely getting an A-minus in one of my classes. Probably AP Lang. Not horrific, not enough to get rescinded from college.

"I don't know. I don't really care about school these days, to be honest."

"Senioritis got to you, too?" Ingrid's dad jokes.

"Yeah." My laugh is brittle. We can both pretend that's the reason. "Guess so."

"I hear it's all promposal season out there now," Ingrid's mom says. She reaches for another slice of pizza. "Are you going with anyone?"

"No, I don't think I'm going at all."

Ingrid's mom reaches across the table. "You holding up okay, honey?"

I shrug. I feel tears at the corners of my eyes, but I can't cry every time I go over to their house. "I miss her," I whisper. "I just can't imagine doing anything these days without her, so I don't want to do them at all."

"Oh, sweetheart." Her mom squeezes my hand. "We feel that way, too." She sighs. "We were going to go to Peru this summer. After graduation."

"Right. You guys were going to climb Machu Picchu." Ingrid had been so excited about it. She'd shown me her workout routine. Her PowerPoint slides to help convince her parents. She'd been practicing her high school Spanish, too.

"I don't even know if we should go at this point." Her dad sighs. "It feels wrong to go without her."

"I think she'd want you to," I encourage them. "For her."

"Yeah," Ingrid's mom says through a teary smile. "I do, too."

We sit in silence for a moment.

"There's a new development with the autopsy, by the way," Ingrid's dad says.

I lean forward. "The results came back?"

"Preliminary ones did. They suspect she could have had some foreign substance in her system. They're running more tests to be conclusive."

This changes everything. This is definitive evidence. "She was . . . drugged at this party?" I whisper out the last part.

Mrs. Mitchell swallows and nods.

"When do we find out for sure?"

"These things could take a few months," Ingrid's dad replies.

"Too long. Whoever did it could be off to college by then."

"That's the thing," Ingrid's mom says. "We don't know if it was motivated or not. I've been trying to ask around to see if anyone else was drugged at that party, but parents don't really want to talk to me. And that family who hosted the party never responded to our messages. They've only emailed us through their lawyers."

"Which is even more suspicious." I chew on my lip, tear a piece of skin off. Immediately I taste metal. So many questions.

I wish Dalton didn't break up with me. I don't think he would even want to talk to me through a lawyer.

My second thought is that I should tell Jackie all of this.

Mrs. Mitchell's eyes cut over to mine. "You think so? You think Dalton had something to do with it?"

"I don't know. They didn't talk at the party. Not that I know of."

"They're just uptight lawyers who refuse to speak to us unless they have to," Ingrid's dad says. "Celia Burke certainly is that type."

"You know his mom?"

"We'd occasionally cross paths," Ingrid's mom says. "Back when she was the legal counsel at Bracken. Sometimes she'd bring Dalton around. He always seemed like a sweet kid. Very bright." She leans back. "But it could have been anyone at that party. Do you think someone"—her voice breaks—"wanted to hurt her?"

Her face crumples and she starts sobbing. Instinctively, I reach for her. I hold her for a long time, very tightly. *I don't know*, I want to answer, but I'm not sure that's the truth.

I'm in Ingrid's room, kneeling on the carpet. The wall is covered in soft string lights. We'd painted these walls together, this beautiful, soft, soothing lavender color, when we were twelve. Her dad had helped us tape the corners. There's a lingering floral scent—that's the Daisy by Marc Jacobs rollerball I got her as a present for Christmas. There is her vision board, with styles she loved and wanted to imitate. There is the brand of lipstick she was obsessed with because her favorite influencer wore it. She would spend hours in front of a mirror sometimes, putting on a full face, deciding she didn't like it, and taking it all off and trying again. She was really into skin care, because she had acne scars from Accutane and felt insecure about it.

There is her photo wall. Pictures with her cousins. Pictures with her theater cast from last year when they did *West Side Story*. The one picture of me and Ingrid on the board is from sophomore year, after it seemed like she'd been avoiding me for a while because she was really trying to get close to the poms group. There were always times when it seemed like she'd decided she'd outgrown me. But then she got cut out of one of her supposed friends' birthday parties, and then their homecoming group altogether. Ingrid called me, crying, and I immediately went over to her house and I knew that we were good again.

Instead of homecoming we went to a Maggie Rogers concert, one that Ingrid's parents paid for because they felt so bad for her. We dressed up and Ingrid had meticulously straightened her auburn curls. We went downtown and spent the whole day by the water. We got sushi and Ingrid put it on the new shiny debit card she'd just gotten. We walked to Petco Park on a warm September evening that was just cooling down, and when the wind picked up, Ingrid draped her oversize jean jacket over our shoulders. The tiny figure of Maggie Rogers skipped onto the stage, beaming up at us through the Jumbotron screens, her sheer gossamer dress fluttering in the breeze. And as the sky darkened and the lights came on, she sang "Love You for a Long Time" and Ingrid hugged me, so close I could hear her heart beating against mine. She mouthed the words to me and I plummeted into happiness. I was always aware, but it crystallized then how lucky I was to be loved by her, how lucky I was that she'd chosen me. How I would do anything for her because of it. I was her sidekick in this life, and I always would be.

Now I lie on her soft rug under her string lights. The blank white ceiling is the only thing devoid of color in this room. Her heart necklace settles around my neck. I know I should return it to her—or to this room, rather—but part of me is selfish and wants to keep her as close to me as possible.

Her clothes are neatly folded on the bed. Her parents had done that for her, I'm sure, because she was never good at cleaning up after herself. Sometimes her floor would get so messy that you couldn't see this rug because it was covered in her clothes, and I'd come over and clean it up for her. I was always good at taking care of her. I carried allergy meds in my backpack during the spring in case her pollen allergies flared up, knew to bring Ben & Jerry's Half Baked ice cream when she was feeling sad, calmed her down late at night for hours, helped her make her college vision board. None of her other friends—not her theater cast, not Jackie—knew her from the beginning, knew her every version, the transformations she put herself through, the hobbies she took on and the selves she became. I did.

At eye level, I see her backpack is still open. A trigonometry test flutters out with a B-minus mark on it. Behind that, there's her school Chromebook.

I sit up. Suddenly, I have an idea: I can't log in to her phone, but I've studied with Ingrid enough times to know the password to her school laptop. And she's logged in to her personal email via her school laptop.

Her computer feels light, cold to the touch. I plug it in and power it on. It wakes up from sleep; it was never shut down. Her school password is unchanged: Loki14. Before I know it, I'm in. I pull up my phone and log out of my iCloud account. I type in her email and click Forgot Password. Five seconds later, I get what I'm waiting for: An email pops into her inbox on her school laptop.

Hands shaking, I reset her password. It sends a code to this email, again, and I enter it.

And I'm truly in.

When everything's been synced, I go straight to her texts. The first messages I see are her parents' increasingly frantic texts up top in the pinned group chat.

12:30 A.M.

Mom

Hey sweetie, you made it to Amelia's?

9:30 A.M.

Text me when you wake up. Why is your location turned off?

9:45 A.M.

Tried calling you. All going to voicemail. Call me ASAP or I'm going to call Amelia.

Farther down, there are my texts to her that night, asking if I can pick her up, and then the worried ones the next morning. At midnight, I see Dana, one of her theater friends, has texted asking where she's gone and if she wants to take another round of Jell-O shots. I keep scrolling.

One other person texted her that night.

Jackie Anh.

CHAPTER FOURTEEN

8:45 P.M.

Jackie

Okay, thoughts on this latest ep of Yellowjackets??? I feel so ill about it

What are you up to tonight?

8:49 P.M.

Also, this is between us, but I was talking to Will today and he said that he's telling people he wants to ask me to prom?

9:03 P.M.

Ingrid

oh shit will yoon from chem?

Sadly as predicted, yes

Ugh

I feel like I need to let him down gently but I don't know what to say?

9:36 P.M.

Ingrid

ok but like honestly if he's the only prom ask you have at this point you might as well just say yes. Like fuck it u know

at least u have a prom date

Jackie

I'd honestly rather go to prom with you than with Will

9:45 P.M.

Also . . . did I see Cody texting you today?

ugh it's a whole thing

9:57 P.M.

What are you doing tonight? Do you want to come to mine and watch a movie? We can unpack everything about Cody and Will

Also like no pressure, but I want to talk to you about something

what is it

is something up with newspaper? dude it's a Friday night

is this about your parents again

Jackie

Oh no, not about my dad even. Though he's being kind of an asshole right now.

no worries it's like not newspaper related but I just had some things I wanted to tell u in person? It's not urgent or anything but it's kind of something I've been wanting to talk to you about for a while

Ingrid

??? are u mad at me???

No!!! No not at all

I didn't mean to scare you it's like not an issue or a big deal at all, I was just hoping we can hang out tonight but we can totally do it later

10:43 P.M.

hiiii

ok lets talk

come to this party!!

Wait what?

ugh kinda wanna tell u smth too but maybe when I see u in school monday

Where are you?

Jackie

Do u need me to come? Do u need a ride back?

Ingrid

no no just come we'll chat

jwllo shots

at this St. Anthony's kids house dropping u my location

Okay! coming

Jackie went to Dalton's party. That I knew, but I never knew that she had talked to Ingrid. She never brought it up, not in any of our conversations. This never made it onto the insanely detailed, color-coded timeline. In fact, she had said she never saw Ingrid. Right? Did I remember this correctly?

She was lying.

I try hard to remember my first conversation with her about this. She came around eleven and said that she left around eleven twenty. That is a very narrow window of time, and one that I'm now questioning. If—and this is now a very big *if*—Jackie was truthful about this, they would have hung out at the party after Ingrid and I talked. Before I made out with Aditya and Jackie saw us together. But why would Jackie lie to me about whether she'd talked to Ingrid? What had Jackie needed to tell her that she didn't—or wouldn't—tell me about? Were they in a fight? Whatever they spoke about, it could be key to figuring out exactly where Ingrid went.

The timeline goes dark after midnight. Technically, Ingrid talked to Max and Pat Hayden after she talked to Jackie. But still, Jackie was one of the last people to see and speak to Ingrid before she disappeared.

My head spins. Jackie's words echo back to me. *Murders are often committed by someone the victim knows.*

I shake my head in Ingrid's empty room. I *knew* Jackie was bad news.

She is a suspect now. Could *she* have been involved in Ingrid's death? Faked an investigation so no one else could get to it first? Could this all be an elaborate ruse on her end? I mull over this possibility as I say goodbye to Ingrid's parents and go home.

Hours drag into midnight, and then into dawn.

I've sat so still and hunched in my bed that I'm beginning to lose circulation. What are the plausible scenarios here? She went to the party around eleven. Stayed for a minute to talk to Ingrid about something, and then left the party. But did she truly leave, or did she meet up with Ingrid sometime after midnight? Jackie was obsessed with figuring out the exact time Ingrid left. But in all of her careful interrogations, she never directed them toward herself.

That's the other point of confusion in this hypothesis. Why *would* she start this investigation? Did she do it to control the narrative? Did she want to get ahead of any theories, since she was the so-called true crime expert? Maybe she wanted to put on a show, dig around a little, and declare the case closed.

And the most important question: What was her motive here? She and Ingrid were friends, or at least appeared to have been. Did they have a fight? Did Jackie secretly hate Ingrid? I just need to know what they talked about in that conversation. And unfortunately, I can only find that out from one person.

The next morning, practically immobilized by my anxiety and paranoia, I pull a career first and ask my mom to call me out of school. Too much has happened this weekend, between the two breakups, the implosion of whatever fragile alliance Jackie and I had, and the revelation of her texts. I don't even know if I'm faking this illness all that much. Whatever it is—the heartbreak, the grief, the lack of sleep—must be seriously manifesting in my body, because when my mother puts a hand to my forehead she says I'm feeling hot and look really pale. She makes another huge batch of goji berry tea before she goes to bed.

I go back into my room. At some point I tip into a fraught sleep. When I wake up, it's four in the afternoon. Max hasn't texted me yet, which gives me a semblance of hope that's mixed with fear. Any moment the other shoe will drop. It's far, far too quiet. Even the texts from Jackie have stopped. I feel the immediate urge to drive to school and confront her. But school is already over. I've lost my chance. I tell myself that it can wait until tomorrow and then realize that it can't. I need to talk to Jackie now.

I still have the address saved from when I was going to go over to her house. It's not far from mine. I put on my running clothes and grab a hat. My mom brightens when I emerge in workout gear. "You feel better?"

I nod. "Much, much better."

She claps her hands. "I *knew* it. Goji berry tea always fixes everything." She ladles me another cup. "Oh! I wanted to talk to you about something."

Dread seizes every molecule of my being.

"I was looking at places around San Francisco."

I slurp on my tea and stare at her blankly. "What for?"

"Well—I figure that you're moving to Berkeley, so I could follow you and be nearby. I could sell this place. Housing prices are up in San Diego, you know. We could make a good profit."

"What about your job at the hotel?"

"I could get another one. I'm tired of working at this one. Maybe I could even do something else. I've been thinking about getting my real estate license."

"Real estate license? I thought you always wanted to go to school for architecture."

"Yes, but . . . that costs too much money. I need a degree. A real estate license is more practical."

"And you're going to do that in San Francisco? You haven't even lived there."

"Wouldn't it be nice? I could bring you food. You could come home for the weekends."

So we're just going to leave San Diego altogether? Leave behind everything I've ever known? The prospect is dizzying. "Mom, it's literally an hour flight from San Francisco to here. I'm not going to be far from you. You don't need to follow me everywhere."

Her hopeful expression drops and I suddenly feel bad as I realize this is all because she's scared of being lonely next year.

It's been just us for so long, and she devoted all her free time to raising me. What will happen when I leave? Sure, she has her acquaintances in this city from the church she goes to, but even that's not much. I had wanted to be able to help her out with going back to college, but even that's in jeopardy now.

"We can talk about this later, okay?" I smile to reassure her and force myself out the door before I chicken out.

My legs move of their own accord and I'm flying down the street, in an almost nervous, rocky sprint. I slow down. Once I am in motion there is no going back. I wish I'd grabbed sunglasses. What if I run into Dalton? I feel like a criminal on the run. At this point, I'm surprised that Dalton's mom hasn't served me papers taking me to small claims court. But maybe he hasn't said a thing. Maybe the embarrassment of having a fake girlfriend is strong enough mutually assured destruction to keep his mouth shut.

I jog up and down the hills and up Ivanhoe Avenue. I get a stitch that pinches my side and then remember to breathe deeply and push through. When I did cross-country, we would do a five-mile run each day after school, and halfway through the run my mind would start feeling calmer as we ran past the cliffs. Now it still feels soothing to move my body somewhat, but I'm wracked with errant thoughts. Why do rich people live on hills? Why does the sidewalk just randomly end at some houses? I get that people want uninterrupted lawns, but haven't they thought about the possibility of witnessing vehicular manslaughter on their curbside? I play stop-sign chicken with a few Teslas, and finally I'm in front of a squarish white bungalow. Cute, but a little nondescript. I check my Notes app to see if this matches the address I looked up.

Glancing back at the house, I spot Jackie in the window. She's pacing around, chewing on her thumbnail. My mind tumbles through all these possibilities—her and Ingrid talking at Dalton's party. Her following Ingrid from the party and to the cliffs. Jackie and Ingrid shouting over the wind at each other. Jackie giving Ingrid a violent push. That's a plausible story, right?

Suddenly I feel strange about this. What, I'm just going to show up to her door and demand answers? Jackie knows all about true crime; she would know how to cover her tracks. Better that I retreat right now. Maybe I can continue to avoid her, ask around at school to see if anyone had seen Jackie and Ingrid talking at the party.

While I'm thinking through this, the door opens.

It's too late to leave without being seen. I launch myself behind a bush, bracing myself to see Jackie, but it's just her mom taking the dog out. The dog presses in my direction for a moment, but Jackie's mom is too busy looking at her phone. She pulls on the leash, taking them the other way.

I tense at my close call. It's already too weird of a place to be caught. I straighten up to leave and then suddenly a car pulls up in the driveway. Jackie's looking out of her window. I keep my painful squat behind the bush, contorting myself to stay out of sight. A man steps out of a Subaru. Is this Jackie's dad, then? He's facing the front door. If I slipped out right now, would he notice?

The door opens. Jackie says, "I don't want to see you here."

Shoot. I can't leave now.

"Jack," her dad says gently. "Come on. I just want to talk."

"You don't deserve to come around here. Where's your *girlfriend*?"

"Hey. Don't be difficult. I was just in the neighborhood and thought I'd stop by. You weren't replying to any of my texts."

Interesting. What's going on? Neither of us are very forthcoming with each other. I just know she wasn't really getting along with her dad. I shift positions, my thighs burning, and listen closer.

"I didn't want to."

"It doesn't have to be like this. Just come have dinner with me."

"Is your child bride going to be there?"

"Yes." A sigh. "She's almost thirty, Jack."

"Yeah. An infant."

I am *definitely* intruding on something I should not be.

"I want you guys to get along. It would all be easier if you weren't so difficult, you know? We're both happier now, your mom and me. Can't you see that?"

Jackie doesn't say anything. She just crosses her arms. "Mom's coming back home soon. I wonder what she'll make of that."

"Just ice cream then. Like we used to?"

Suddenly there is a whir, and the sprinkler starts, and I get struck with a spray of water. I emit a yelp and jump to the left to avoid the direct spray. Jackie and her dad both look in my direction. And I'm ejected from the hedge onto their lawn, ass on grass, soaked.

Jackie's jaw drops. "What the fuck?"

I get up and run. I sprint down the lawn, down the driveway, and down the hill I huffed and puffed my way up. I go down so fast I trip, and I go flying. I pick myself up, scrapes and all, and keep running.

CHAPTER FIFTEEN

I can't fake being sick again the next day because I have two tests to take. Despite everything that's happened, my grades are still decent, except for AP Lang. That *Macbeth* paper is going to be the death of my valedictorian dream. It also doesn't help that I'm on very weird terms with the person who's supposed to be writing my paper with me.

I do very much need to confront Jackie about the texts. On the drive there, I try to think of how I should approach her. Do I take her aside before school starts? Try to catch her walking out from class? Turns out, I don't even need to give it much thought, because she locks gazes with me in the hallway. Her large brown eyes narrow, and I'm terrified. She hunts me down right before I go into first period AP Calc.

"I need answers from you."

So do I. The bell rings. I glance at the door. "I need to go in for this test."

She doesn't even take a breath. "Why were you on my lawn yesterday? Why did you not respond to any of my texts? And that doesn't even scratch the surface of what happened with Dalton? Like—"

"Can we . . . not talk about this at school?" I look around. "I will explain everything. I promise."

Her voice only rises. "Stop being avoidant."

The Calc teacher hovers by the door and shoots me a pointed look. I face Jackie head-on and look her level in the eyes. "I'm not being avoidant. I just need to take this test, or else I'll have ditched too many classes, and I really don't want to hash this out with you in after-school detention. Okay?"

"Fine. I'll come find you at lunch." Jackie narrows her eyes again. "Wait. We have different lunch periods today. I'm going to come find you after AP Psych."

How did she know that about our lunch periods? "Jeez. Don't threaten me with a good time."

"This *is* a threat, actually. I'll see you there." Jackie marches away in a huff, her nylon tote swinging from her shoulder.

I go in and slog through a calc test that makes me wish I never came in. I'm generally pretty quick to get things in math, especially when it comes to data and stats, but this is verging on abstract multivariable calculus and matrices, and I have been so fully checked out the past few weeks. For the first time, I have no idea what I'm looking at, and I'm actually fearing that I'll fail and Berkeley might rescind my acceptance. I squirm through my three other classes in a trance, eat my lunch in the empty theater auditorium Ingrid so loved, and wonder what I'm going to say to Jackie later. Am I going to bring up the texts? I should give her a chance to explain herself, shouldn't I? But that's just the start.

What is she going to ask *me*? I didn't have the guts to look at her texts. If I'm going to be torn apart in questioning, better that it happen all at once.

I also wonder about Max. Has he not texted me because he

found out the truth about my ruse and he won't speak to me? Did Dalton and Aditya track him down? There's no way—none of my fake selves connect to one another. I made sure that they went to different schools, had separate friend circles. Does he not have text access in Hong Kong? Or maybe no one has told him yet? My saving grace is that he actually doesn't know that many people in La Jolla. Max has friends from his school, but he's not particularly close to them, since he only moved here a year ago. He feels out of place, that's for sure, but he doesn't really care, because he mostly travels and does his film stuff outside of school, anyway.

As promised, Jackie is waiting by my AP Psych classroom at three thirty on the dot. I stare warily at her. "You're waiting like an overeager boyfriend."

"Should I call you Amy, then?"

"Fuck off." I march toward the doors.

"You know, my dad actually wanted to call the cops on you yesterday. I told him not to."

My face goes red at the mention of me on Jackie's lawn. How could one person cause me inordinate levels of embarrassment just in the past week? It makes me wish I'd never approached Jackie in the first place to figure out what happened to Ingrid. I could just as well have made exactly the same amount of progress on my own.

"Well, isn't that kind," I snipe.

"I think if you're quite literally trespassing on my property, you kind of owe me an explanation."

We're finally at my car. I sigh. "Fine. Let's talk." I nod at her. "Get in."

"Whoa. What's happening? Why are you making me get into your car? Are you going to take me to a second location?"

"Can you stop overthinking things? I just want to talk with some privacy. Can we at least have that?"

Jackie hesitates, and then she gets into my passenger seat. She frowns at all the things I have in my car. I notice at the last second that there is a sheer corset top that I've shoved into the glove box. I don't even want to begin to unpack that. She glances at me with a question in her eyes, and then quickly looks away, her cheeks coloring with a faint blush. She tucks her cropped hair behind her ears. My cheeks feel hot, too. "You drive stick?"

"Yeah," I say. "This was my dad's car. He drove stick, so I learned to."

"That's . . . that's kind of cool, actually."

"Have I redeemed myself in your eyes?" I say, my voice laced with sarcasm.

"Absolutely not. You're still suspicious."

"All right, an interrogation. Sounds fun."

"Why were you stalking me?" Jackie quickly asks.

"Okay, that phrasing is a little *strong*."

"You," she reasons, "were hiding in my hydrangea bushes, so if you can come up with a more accurate term, I'll take it."

I sigh. "I didn't mean to end up there."

"Oh, you just wandered into my sprinkler system."

"Fine. I was . . ." I pause. "You know what, I'm going to explain myself, I promise, but I'm going to ask you about something first."

Jackie turns so she faces me, jabbing a finger at me. "*No.* No.

You have not earned that right. I have a million questions that you're going to answer first before I even get to your question."

"This one comes first," I insist. "I went to your house because I wanted to ask you about the texts you sent Ingrid the night of the party. But then your dad pulled up, and, I don't know, you guys seemed to be having kind of an uncomfortable conversation."

"Yeah. He's a cheater, but we don't need to get into all that. Also, wait. What texts?"

A *cheater*? I need to revisit this. I hold up my phone. "I hacked into Ingrid's iCloud."

Jackie's eyes grow wide. "You *what*? Hold on. Is that even legal?"

"Why not? Also, that's not the point. You said we needed information. This was just a means to more information."

"I'm pretty sure when it involves hacking into a dead person's phone, the means are pretty relevant!"

I was going to wait to let Jackie explain herself. But based on her hesitance, I know she's not going to, at least not without me questioning her. "You were one of the last people to text Ingrid. You were going to have a conversation with her." I stop talking and hold up the phone. Jackie tries to swipe it from me but I move it away. "Why didn't you tell me this?"

Jackie crosses her arms. Her gaze flickers to the phone. Finally, she is at a loss for words. I don't take my eyes off her. How she reacts to this will give me critical information. "It was just a side conversation," she finally says. "It wasn't important."

"*You* were the one who said we should talk to everyone at

this party who'd interacted with her. All this time and you never said anything?" I press forward. We're inches away. Jackie's face contorts into a look of shock. Her cheeks redden and her eyes dart around—out of fear or anger, I can't tell.

"I liked her!" she blurts. "Okay?"

I falter. "What?"

Jackie buries her face in her hands. "I don't know. I just really liked her, and I thought she was really cool and sweet, and really pretty, and I just developed this . . . raging, inconvenient crush on her, and I wanted to tell her how I felt, so . . . I don't know, I could—you know, deal with it, or get over it, or . . ."

"You . . . had *feelings* for Ingrid?"

"Yeah." Jackie swallows hard. "We got close during newspaper. She had this whole thing where I couldn't really tell if she was flirting with me or not. And I had a whole speech prepared, and I was agonizing over it for a few days to the point where I knew that I wanted to confess my feelings to her. But then she told me to show up to this party, and I was like, okay, maybe we could, like, be honest, and if she was drunk and rejected me she'd . . . I don't know. Forget about it." Jackie shakes her head, but it's more at herself than at me. "But then I went and there were too many people and I got really overwhelmed. So I left. And I never really told her what I wanted to say, and now I'll never get the chance, so it doesn't really matter, okay?" Jackie pulls something up on her phone. "This is my whole speech. I have proof. It's time-stamped from that night."

I grab for it and she holds it out of reach. "You don't have to actually read it."

She flicks the screen and scrolls through the whole thing.

"Jackie, this is an essay."

"I wasn't soliciting writing feedback, but noted," Jackie says sharply. "I just had a lot to say."

"I mean that this is impressive." I lean back. "That's . . . it? Just a confession?"

"Essentially."

"Why didn't you tell me?"

"It's embarrassing to crush on a girl who's probably straight."

I laugh. "Oh my god, Jackie, I was worried. It's just that?"

"What, you thought I was a suspect? You thought I *killed* her?" Jackie leans back, too, so we are parallel to each other. Her eyes narrow and scrutinize mine. "You really thought that."

Now that I really think about it, maybe my theory was a little far-fetched. "I was doing what you would have done. I was being diligent."

"Well, then. Speaking of people who hide things. I've answered your question. Now you need to tell me everything. I'm not letting you leave this car until you answer every single question I have."

I sigh and pick up a gum wrapper that has fallen into the crevice of my cupholder. Crushing the foil in my hands, I pinch and roll it between my fingers until it forms a smooth ball. "Well, since I'm being held in my own car against my will . . . what do you want to know?"

"You were dating Dalton Burke," Jackie asserts.

I nod reluctantly.

"You were dating him under a fake name. You were also dating Aditya Kalra at the same time. So you were cheating on both of them."

"Technically."

"*Literally.* The act of cheating is literally the act of being deceptive and unfaithful in a relationship."

"Yes. Fine." I sigh. "If you want to *dictionary* me, I was in a relationship with each of them. I cheated on both of them. But it was intentional. And it's not as bad as it sounds."

"Granted, Dalton is an asshole," Jackie reasons. "But still, it's morally unethical. And as you now know because of the stuff with my dad, I *hate* cheaters. What's wrong with you?"

Jackie's pinned me with a sharp, deadpan stare. There's no other way out of this. I have to tell the truth.

"I planned it with Ingrid," I finally confess. "We came up with it together."

"*What?*"

"You want to hear the full story?"

"Of course."

"Okay," I relent. "It's going to be a long one. Can we go somewhere?"

"Where?"

"It's all going to make sense," I tell her. "I promise. We're just going down the road—to the headquarters of Bracken Pharmaceuticals."

I drive us down the winding road, past a grove of trees. A tall, imposing brutalist building rises in front of us, made of nondescript sandy brick. It looks like a huge LEGO block. The windows are minimal and tinted blue. We're in a mostly empty gated parking lot. Before us is the disposal station. I park, and we jolt a little bit as I shift the clutch into place.

"I'm not sure I like this." Jackie scrunches her nose. "Why'd you take us to Bracken's dead-end dumpster?"

"Because no one will come back here." I roll down the window an inch and unclip my seat belt. "I don't even know where to start. Okay. It's not really about the boys."

Jackie gives me a bewildered look. "Are there more boys? How many boys are you—defrauding?"

"There's another one."

Her eyebrows disappear behind her bangs. "You're simultaneously swindling *three boys*?"

"Yeah. Max Bracken is the third."

"Bracken." Jackie turns and looks at the building, and then back at me. "The Bracken Pharma kid?"

I lean forward. "Exactly. This is about their parents." I point up at the building. "This is going to be about Bracken Pharmaceuticals. And my missing dad."

Jackie sits up, chewing on the inside of her cheek. "What happened to your dad?"

"My dad worked for Bracken Pharma for years and it ruined our lives."

Jackie folds her legs up to her chest. Her eyes are wide.

I pause to carefully think through what I'm going to say next. "I've never really told anyone this story. Well, except Ingrid. But, um. The story is my dad worked for the research group of Bracken Pharmaceuticals. He was working on this heart medication with them. It was, like, a platelet inhibitor. Paloxene was the name." I pause, fiddling with my—Ingrid's—necklace. "And the thing was my dad had been researching this kind of thing all his life, because my grandmother died of heart disease when he was young. So he'd done a doctorate on hypertension populations and he believed that this drug could work. And so he was one of the founding members behind this research group. That's the whole reason why my family settled in San Diego."

"Makes sense," Jackie says. "Seems like everyone's parent works for Bracken Pharmaceuticals. It basically runs the city."

"Yeah. So my dad was working on this medication that he thought would decrease the risk of a heart attack or a stroke, and he'd researched this for years and he worked on a team, and so they finally got FDA approval. Like, it was exciting. I mean, he'd done it, right? He'd done what he wanted to his entire life. And this medicine launched, and it was making a ton of money, and so he got promoted. That's when everything changed."

"I'm hearing a lot of past tense in this story," Jackie interjects. "Is your dad—"

"Let me finish," I interrupt. "I think it was around . . . seven or eight years ago at this point? He realized that something was wrong with the results of the clinical trial study. He realized that people were getting stomach bleeds. At this point he was overseeing the research part of this, but he wasn't in charge of the FDA approval cycle or anything. So he looks into this, and here's the thing: He discovered that his team had been *making numbers up*."

"So this heart medication . . . didn't work?"

"It didn't work," I confirm. "But it was worse than that. He discovered that people were suffering from stomach bleeds at a disproportionate rate, and people were dying from these stomach bleeds. And Bracken was covering it up."

I glance at the dumpsters through the windshield.

"I was eleven years old by the time he finally gathered enough evidence to raise it as an issue," I say hollowly. "I remember him talking to my mom about it. It didn't make any sense to me at the time. I didn't even know what whistleblowing was at that age, or just how insanely hard it was to go up against a company that wanted to do everything in its power to silence you. But he spoke out about it. He tried to take it to his direct research team, but they didn't listen to him. I just remember . . ." I fold my hands in my lap. "He was so sad during that time, and he didn't talk to anyone, and all he did was stay in his office. He used to take me places on the weekends. Like to the beach. Or to a baseball game. He loved baseball, and he'd drive me hours to see a Dodgers game because that was his favorite team. But he stopped doing that. It was like his entire personality had shifted." I close my eyes, press the pads of my fingertips to my eyelids. I try to fight back tears. "And then he started becoming paranoid. He told me someone was coming for him. People were following him. He said his phone was being bugged. He was getting intimidation notices in the mail. People were filing lawsuits against the company, and they asked him to be a part of it to testify."

I look up at the imposing company building. I see through the windows that people are moving about at their desks, with no sign of slowing down. They look so small from this vantage point.

"The last day he was here, he took me to the movies," I whisper. "That Edwards movie theater in Mira Mesa. And then he took me to 99 Ranch, that Asian grocery store, and he told me I could get whatever snacks I wanted, and then he took me to lunch after, just the two of us. We had hand-pulled noodles in this restaurant in Convoy. And then we went to the beach, and we ate those snacks on the beach. I had jelly candies and panda crackers until I got sick." I remember that day. The day before he left. The perfect, stunning clarity of it. It's a day I have dreamed about, that I have walked through a million times. "We came home and he had to pack to fly out to be deposed for this lawsuit." I sniff. "He flew out the next morning. He never came back."

"Ever?" Jackie whispers.

"I don't know what happened to him. There are several possibilities, right? Either Bracken didn't want him revealing the information in that court case and they did something to him . . . or maybe he had a breakdown somewhere and left. He left us one note that my mom found later. He said that he was scared for himself and scared for us and he wanted to do whatever he could to protect us. I don't know if he's alive or if—if he did something to himself, or someone did something to him, or . . ." My voice shakes. My heart is hammering and my cheeks flush. "And Bracken was really good at covering the case up. Whatever my dad discovered, there was no way to search for it again. There was never any confirmation or sighting. That's the worst part. The case disappeared and my dad was just . . . gone. And I've spent the past six years thinking about what I could have done. How I could have kept him around."

"You couldn't have done anything," Jackie says firmly. "He was trying to be a whistleblower. I can only imagine how insanely difficult that was. He was up against—this machine of a company that just wanted to make a profit at the expense of other people."

I nod and sigh. "You're right. Which takes us to the three boys."

"Dalton, Aditya, and Max."

I lean forward, my pointer finger hovering in the air. "Max Bracken's dad is the CEO of Bracken Pharmaceuticals. He played a key role in the cover-up." I draw an invisible arrow. "Dalton Burke's mom is Celia Burke. Before she became congress-woman of our district, she was the key in-house lawyer who sent my dad the cease and desist letters. Made his life hell. She harassed him until he felt like he couldn't even be safe around his own family anymore. And Aditya Kalra's dad, who was the head of R&D, used to be my dad's friend. He turned my dad in and was the one who got him fired when my dad started expressing all these doubts to him about the misrepresented harms of that drug."

I lean back. "So because of these three people, my family was ruined. I never get to see my dad again, all because he saw people dying from this drug and decided to speak up. But these three? They covered it all up and got away with it." An edge creeps into my voice. "And their families are so fucking *wealthy*, Jackie."

"I am painfully aware of that."

"None of them ever faced consequences. The case was dismissed. And they continue to live their lavish lives and make more money in a year than any of us will ever see in our lifetimes. They got away with it." I stare up at the bland sandstone walls and try to imagine what's inside the fortress. "I think about it, you know. What could have happened if—if someone did something about it. I wanted to look into the case. I wanted information, and I wanted revenge. And the best way to get both was through dating their sons."

"And so *that*," Jackie says slowly, "is how you ended up with three boyfriends."

"I wanted to know what their lives were like," I explain. "I wanted to see if there was, you know, a way to access information. If only I was in their homes, and in their lives, and got the trust of the parents who had ruined my dad's life, I thought I could, you know, say whatever and make up whatever stories I could about myself in order to convince them of their trust. To make them like me. Of course I wasn't honest. Sometimes they gave me these extravagant gifts and I'd return them and get some money. Sometimes I would make up a story about a start-up I was doing to get fake seed funding. Ingrid and I also planned to pool some of the money we got from them and donate to nonprofits that benefit people with stomach bleeds. I put a part of it toward a fund for my mom, because she wants to go back to college." I lift my chin. "I know you're judging me. But I thought it would be a way to get back at them. For, you know, what they did."

Jackie stares at me for a long minute. "It's sweet," she finally says. "That you're thinking of your mom like this."

I relax slightly.

"But this is seriously, seriously illegal. It's, like, ten different kinds of fraud."

My stomach drops. She's taking this all down as a confession. I bet there's a hidden recorder in her pocket. All this vulnerability and she's going to narc on me?

"But I don't . . . actually hate it." Jackie eyes me thoughtfully. "It's, like . . . vigilante justice. You're a modern-day Robin Hood."

"That's the nicest thing you've ever said to me."

She rolls her eyes. "Don't be flattered. My irritation with you is marginally outweighed by my distaste for evil billionaires." She pauses and I can almost see her mind furiously working. "This is, like, the stuff of a massive exposé that they'd publish in *The Washington Post* or something. Did you ever find any evidence of what they did?"

I slump in my seat and shake my head. "No. I didn't. It was almost impossible to find something that far back. Also, two out of three sources of intel dumped me. So."

"Okay, I'm sorry for exposing you," Jackie says. "But I was operating on imperfect information. What, I should have just guessed that you were cheating in a plot of class consciousness and corporate revenge?"

"You could have asked."

"You weren't exactly being forthcoming."

"Neither were you."

Jackie goes quiet. "Fair."

We both look out the windshield.

"You know," Jackie finally says. "Maybe we don't have to like each other that much. But we could still . . . learn to trust each other."

Trust. That I can get behind. "Yeah," I say, meeting her eyes as she turns to look at me. "Well, thank you for telling me about Ingrid. That means a lot to me."

"And thank you for telling me about your dad." Jackie bites her lip. "And . . . everything."

"I figured I'd tell you the truth at some point or another," I reply. "But I'm sorry for being weird about it. I didn't mean to stalk you, I promise. I just wanted to talk to you in person."

"All good." Jackie laughs. "Now that I know this was for an ethically good cause." She crosses her arms. "We're even?"

"Guess we are."

Jackie nods curtly and peers around her. "What a place to have a heart-to-heart."

I forgot that we're still in the dumpster lot of Bracken. "Oh. Yeah. Also, sorry. I didn't mean to keep you from your plans."

"Yeah, it's not a big deal. I just should probably do my edits on my article."

"See, I can't interrupt that fun."

Jackie rolls her eyes. "Does us being even mean you'll at least try to be nicer to me?"

"Not a chance." Buckling my seat belt, I start the car to take her home.

"You know where to go?" Jackie asks with mock concern. "The address is—"

"Shut up."

She rolls her eyes but in a playful, almost Ingrid-like way, and I warm inside. As we begin to head back, Jackie looks at her phone and groans.

"What?"

"My dad's asking if I want to get dinner with him and his girlfriend tonight. Because I blew off dinner with them the other day. Shoot. I need to get out of this."

"You don't want to go?"

"I'm just really annoyed by him right now. This is just how

he always is. Always tries to sweep in at the last second. He couldn't care less about us, and suddenly he's all trying to get involved back in my life. I think he's about to propose to his girlfriend, so he, like, wants us to all cosplay being a fun, cohesive family." Jackie snorts. "I would literally do anything else in the world."

I pass by a taco shop, and I get an idea. "Let's grab dinner."

Jackie looks at me. "What?"

I nod at Don Carlos. "We can get tacos. Or whatever you want. And you can tell him you have to work on a class project. Technically, you'd be telling the truth." I shrug. "If you want." Did I just suggest plans? Am I voluntarily hanging out with her? But she brightens, and it's too late to take back.

"Okay! Yes. *Yes.*" Jackie's fingers fly over the keyboard. Her chest heaves in relief. "Tacos are perfect."

CHAPTER SIXTEEN

"So what happened with your dad? If you don't mind me asking."

Jackie focuses intently on her tacos. We've ended up by the beach, sitting on some rocks above La Jolla Cove. We couldn't eat in the taco shop because it was tiny and crowded and there was only one table, so we made our way here. It's not bad, and the open air and breeze feel nice.

"I probably should be nicer to him." She carefully places the radish pieces on top of her meat. "When I was a kid, we did everything together. He's the smartest person I know. I mean, he'd take me to museums and quiz me after. The entire time, all I thought about was impressing him. Then about . . . my freshman year?" Jackie glances up from her taco and taps her chin. "I saw he'd keep turning his location off at random times. That's when I figured out he was texting his coworker and cheating on my mom." She sighs, narrowing her eyes at the waning sun. "I didn't speak to him for a whole year. And when I did, he kept trying to make it up to me by taking me out to dinner or helping with my college applications. But that doesn't cancel out what he did." Her pursed lips twitch, and she blinks back tears. "And now he's making a new family. I know it's petty, but I refuse to let him feel good about it."

"No, I get it," I say, feeling light-headed, as if I'm reliving Jackie's memories. "I really do. I would feel the same."

"I'm sorry your dad left, too. Even though there was a reason, it wasn't fair to you."

"Thank you." I exhale. I look at her earnestly, at once filled with tenderness, crushed under this unfamiliar magnitude of care for her. Unexpectedly, I put a hand on her arm. "You know, this . . . unraveling. It does get easier over time. Believe me."

She chews on her thumbnail. "It takes me a long time to forgive someone."

"You think you can out-grudge me? I just ran a three-person scam."

"Fair."

"Besides, I didn't say you needed to forgive."

We're quiet for a moment as we eat our tacos. The setting sun bathes us in generous light. I'll miss this place when I leave for college: the clarity of the sky and the precise gradient of colors.

"Do you ever wonder where he is?" Jackie finally asks.

I laugh to myself. "No," I say sarcastically. "It hasn't crossed my mind a single time."

"You've tried looking into it? I mean, yellow pages, phone records, LinkedIn . . ."

"You think I didn't look up his name hundreds of times on the internet? His Chinese name? His family members, to see what had happened? No one knew where he went. At a certain point I thought he was dead, that someone had killed him, and so I looked to see if his name was attached to any case or police department filing. That's how deep I got.

"I stopped trying," I continue. "It's easier pretending he's dead sometimes. I had a whole notebook of things I wrote down that I wanted to say to him when he came back through the front door. But the easiest thing was giving up that possibility that he'd return. He's not coming back. And that way, I never set myself up for disappointment."

"Sorry. Sorry," Jackie mumbles. "I can't even imagine that situation, having no closure. I feel ridiculous for even asking."

I smile wanly at her. "It's okay. I've had six years to process it."

Jackie nods. "Here, have the last taco."

"You should have it."

"No, I insist."

"You don't have to give me a pollo asada taco out of pity for my sob story about my dad."

"Well, I had a fucked-up dad story, too. I just want you to be fed."

"You sound like an Asian grandmother."

Jackie rolls her eyes. "I offer you food and you call me a hag."

"I meant it in a nice way. With great affection."

"Oh. You're no longer just full of hatred for me?"

"I asked you to have dinner on the beach with me." I wave my hands at our surroundings.

"I've made it to the inner circle?"

"It's a very tight circle." I smirk. "There aren't a lot of people in there."

And then Aditya's voice echoes in my ears: *friendless psycho.* The world sharpens into focus as a knot tightens in my throat. "Actually, I can remember the last time I did this with a friend."

"Was it with . . . ?"

"Ingrid? Yeah." I breathe in the salty ocean air. "I had a summer job at the La Jolla Shores Beach Club. Ingrid worked for Bracken that summer. We'd come here after work when we were bored out of our minds. We'd get pizzas and come here. One time we got high after work and brought a whole rotisserie chicken from Pavilions."

Jackie barks out a laugh. "I'm sorry, *what*?"

"Rotisserie chickens are *so* cheap. Perfect for two to share."

"No, I get it. Not that I . . . do that. I can understand. That's just a funny image. She seemed like a fun person to do that with."

"It *was* her idea. As were many things."

"Of course."

"When did you start liking her?" I ask.

Jackie exhales. "I think . . . maybe starting sometime in January? I don't know, I think we first started really talking this year when I took over as editor in chief. But I think we really clicked sometime around, like, Halloween? We both had Reneé Rapp as our most-played Spotify artist, and then we did a Spotify Blend, and then we realized that we actually had a lot in common, and then we were watching this, like, awful and addictive Netflix show, and then she would send me memes about that throughout winter break, and then, just, I don't know. It was really easy to hang out with her, and talk to her, and she was, like, obviously so pretty, and I don't know." Jackie sighs. "For so much of high school I've just been feeling like this . . . to be honest, pretty lonely kid who didn't really have time to socialize because I had all this shit I thought I needed to do in order to get into college, and I thought, you know, it would all start being fun once I got there. But Ingrid made school fun. She was the first person to make me feel like I was actually sort of a cool person."

"Yeah." I smile. "She was good at that."

Jackie raises an eyebrow. "Yeah? I wish I'd met her earlier in high school. I can't believe I only really got to know her senior year." She pauses. "We could have all been a little friend group."

A friend group. I think of Aditya's friends, sprawled over conjoined tables at Raising Cane's. It actually sounds kind of nice.

"When did you guys become friends?" Jackie asks me.

"Third grade," I tell her. "She was the new kid and the teacher assigned us to be partners that first day. I was shy and didn't want to talk to anyone, but she asked me so many questions I had to talk." I bite into my taco. "And then there was a holiday party at our school and we each had to bring a dish. My mom made this sticky Chinese sesame candy, and she cut it into bars, and I brought it in to class. And this boy was mean and said it looked like a turd, and nobody wanted to eat it after that, and I was just at my desk, like, crying and pretending I wasn't, and Ingrid saw. She was the only person who tried it. And she said it was good. We became friends after that. And then our moms volunteered for this one PTA event together, and after that we worked out this carpool schedule where my mom drove us to school and her mom drove us back because my mom worked the three p.m. shift. So I ended up staying over at her house a lot. I think we just . . . fell into it."

"And you were best friends ever since."

"For the most part, yeah." We were friends for ten years. Recent memories unearth in splinters. Her trying on lip stains at Sephora. The two of us smushed together at junior year homecoming, that floral perfume I got for her emanating off her, and her leaning close to me, telling me *You should kiss me* with an eyebrow raised, as if daring me to do it. And of course I did, as I did everything she asked me to. I leaned in and touched my lips softly against hers, so soft I wasn't even sure it was a kiss. We never spoke of it again.

Later, she asked me to help her cheat on a physics test by typing all the answers into her calculator that we passed back and forth. So many times, we slept next to each other, her curls in my face. I won't forget her Herbal Essences shampoo, that blue coconut one, or the mango scent of her curl cream she loved when she finally gave up on straightening her hair.

Is it possible that I liked her, too? The idea sounds silly but until Jackie's confession, I thought only boys could be in love with Ingrid, because Ingrid only liked boys. But I always felt a little irritated when Ingrid talked about her crushes. Maybe a part of me was in love with her, like Jackie.

I don't want to put that into words, so I say quietly, "I just felt like with her, I was . . . chosen. You know? Like you were the only person she felt safe enough to share a secret with. And you didn't know why you were chosen, but you felt lucky that you were."

"That's really lovely," Jackie murmurs.

I stare at the rocks in front of me because I can't look at her.

"You okay?" Jackie asks, brushing my arm. It's a tender

gesture, a touching moment that I ruin by immediately bursting into tears.

I don't know what hits me, but suddenly I'm hunched over, sobbing, and Jackie is patting my back, and handing me napkins, and I'm pressing them to my eyes before recoiling. "Ow. Ow! Lime juice!"

"Oh my god. I'm sorry! I totally forgot."

I laugh as my eyes burn. I laugh because it's like a spell has been broken, the tears a catharsis. Jackie laughs with me, even though she's confused and has no idea what is going on. I recover enough to see again, and I turn to Jackie and sweep her up in a hug. She's stiff in my arms at first, but then she relaxes and wordlessly hugs me back. Thank god she doesn't say anything because I think I'm being so unprecedentedly sincere, I might combust.

"We should have hung out earlier," Jackie says.

"I agree." I sniff. "I'm sorry I was weird this weekend."

"No." Jackie shakes her head. "I mean, like, throughout senior year. I'm discovering that there are all these people I should have gotten to know better, or tried to become friends with, and now we're pretty much out of here and it's too late."

When it finally gets dark, we make our way back to the car. I keep teasing Jackie about trying to blind me and she continues to apologize profusely, holding my arm to steady me. Before we get into the car, I turn to Jackie.

"You know," I say quickly, before I regret it. "There's still over a month of senior year. We have time to be friends."

A beautiful, brilliant smile sweeps across Jackie's cheeks. "Friends. Really?"

"Really."

"So you've just given up on this whole corporate takedown?"

As we near Jackie's house, I glance at my rearview mirror and ease across a hilly intersection. "I'm still technically dating one of the three. But at this point, I feel like it's only a matter of time before he finds out."

"But also, he's, like, *the* Bracken guy, so I feel like you could get a lot of information out of him."

"Yeah." My eyes stay on the road. "I've tried."

"I could help you," Jackie offers. "I might know someone who interned at Bracken Pharma over the summer. Maybe I could see if they know anything."

"Ingrid interned with them, actually," I tell Jackie. "That was the other part of it. She was trying to find me files from the back end. I was using her key card. She got in at a certain point because she had this, like, glitch in her pass that allowed her to access the files, but I think the security system detected her and kicked her out. Nothing really came of that."

"Maybe someone in the company detected her as a threat," Jackie muses.

I come to a sudden halt at the stop sign. "Wait. You're right." I turn at the intersection and pull over to the side of the suburban street.

"What are you doing?"

"I just—I need to think for a second." I click on the hazard lights. "Maybe we've been thinking about this wrong. Maybe the person who came after Ingrid wasn't from high school at all."

"Maybe that person is from Bracken," Jackie whispers. "Maybe they found out she was poking around and they decided to come after her."

"And they decided to . . . ?" The question hangs in the air.

"They could have." Jackie gasps. "After what they did to your dad. You never know. Did anyone ever reach out to her? Harass her?"

"Not to my knowledge. I didn't find anything when I was scrolling her phone." I pause. "Wait. I did want to show you this, though. There was this one text she sent to someone I don't know." It's to an unknown number. It's not saved anywhere within her phone.

Ingrid simply says: Here.

She sent the text at 11:34 p.m. Jackie's brows furrow. I can tell she's scared, too.

"Who is this?" she whispers.

"I don't know. It's not a San Diego area code, that's for sure."

"Okay. Are there more texts than that?"

I scroll her history. "No. There's nothing else."

"Okay, this is a lead. But that means there must have been some kind of communication somewhere else. What about calls? Did she call anyone?"

"Oh, calls. That's a good point. How could I have missed that?" Sloppy, sloppy. The call log holds a lot of what I expect: red missed calls from me, from her mother, from Jackie, from her theater friends as news spread that morning after her disappearance. I scroll to the day of the party. There was one call that morning at 11:31 a.m. The call was four minutes long.

I peer at the number: 212 area code. The last four digits are a pair. Two twos, then two sevens.

"The number matches," Jackie breathes, pointing. "It matches the number of the text." Her eyes widen. She leans close. "Okay. We're on to something. We need to text them." Jackie whips out her phone.

"What—what are you doing? Why are you texting this person?"

"I want to ask them more background questions. Isn't that what we've been doing?"

"What if this person is the killer? They'll know we're on to them."

"Okay. What if we try to trick them?"

I frown. "Trick them how?"

"We do the thing where we text them asking them on a date."

"You want to date this killer? He could be a forty-year-old man."

"No! We do the thing where we ask them on a date, and then they respond that they're not this person, that they're X person. And we have a name."

"Ohhhh. So, yes. The classic scamming move."

"Come on. You should know this." She smirks. "Let's sweetheart-scam the hell out of this murder case."

"Hold on," I say. A 212 area code. Something is coming to me . . . "This is a New York area code."

And I know someone from New York.

I log out of Ingrid's iCloud and log back in to my own. My chest is constricting. An awful, sick feeling fills my stomach. I hope I'm wrong. I certainly don't want to be right. But as I start to type the number in, the contact appears.

"Amelia?" Jackie calls out to me, but her voice sounds faint.

I turn the phone around. "Max Bracken," I whisper at last. "She called him that morning." I know what Jackie's thinking, and I say it for the both of us. "I think he could have been involved with Ingrid's death."

Chapter Seventeen

"Great job, love the leggings, love the shirt—oh, wait!" A senior class cabinet member decked out in the colors of red and yellow stops me in my tracks. "I don't see you wearing *your* spirit on your sleeve!"

Because our school colors are ugly, I want to say, but instead I give him what I hope is an apathetic look and he just lets me pass. I do not care in the least about showing school spirit right now. I am grappling with the fact that Max, of all people, could have been Ingrid's killer.

Turns out, we'd been looking in the wrong places and at the wrong people. Dalton's deleted security camera footage. Ingrid's necklace in Aditya's car. Before this, there was never an apparent reason to suspect my third boyfriend, only his friend Pat. But now, after Jackie and I talked it out last night in my car, the motive couldn't be clearer. Ingrid must have gone to confront Max about the Bracken scandal. He killed her and covered it up.

I follow the crowd to the gym and climb the bleachers all the way to the top, where Jackie's seated far in the corner. I can spot her from her sensible checkered button-down. "You seem annoyed," she observes as I sit next to her.

"Overjoyed, actually. It's the last spirit assembly I have to sit through."

"So Max didn't respond to your text."

I turn. "How'd you know?"

As a response, Jackie reaches out to steady my bouncing leg. "You're irritated and anxious. Clearly."

I sigh. Jackie really can read me. We crafted a text to Max together last night, asking him to go on a date because I missed him so much when he was gone. "The text to him went green. He could have blocked me."

"He might have been on his flight or something."

"It's been ten hours since I sent the text. He would have landed by now. What do we do if he's found out and decided to ghost me, too?"

We both sit in silence for a moment.

Jackie frowns slightly. "Did Ingrid ever tell you what she wanted to confront Max about? Did she learn something terrible or find some piece of evidence?"

I pause. "We had a couple of good leads but no smoking gun. We wanted, like, a report or something. There are a few regulatory documents, but they were password-protected." I exhale, frustrated. "Ingrid wanted to confront Max about it. I told her to wait until we had more conclusive evidence. Maybe she called Max about it that morning. Went to confront him at Dalton's party. And then . . ."

Any thoughts we might have are engulfed by the crackle of the speaker.

"Aaaallll right, Cardinals, who's ready to roll?"

"We need another plan," she calls over the din. "If he's not going to talk to you, what if you reach out to his friend or something. Pat Hayden, right?"

"I mean, I know him through my fake Instagram account. But there's no way I can get him to hang out without him telling Max about it."

"What if you're just straight with it? You tell Pat that you think Max did something to Ingrid that night. Ask to talk to him privately."

"But what if he and Pat were in on it together? Pat is the one we know was talking to Ingrid that night."

We're stuck. If only we had the security footage. If only Dalton hadn't deleted it and blocked me.

"Okay. Let's just get through this assembly and we can talk about it after."

The class president is dancing up on the stage. Teachers are getting pied in the face and I have no idea what is going on, as per usual. The a cappella group is running up the stairs and singing "Uptown Girl." And then Cody Hill, the main soloist of the a cappella group, is unfurling a poster. He approaches Val, who's standing with the theater crew at the sidelines. She beams and throws her arms around him.

A collective gasp ripples through the crowd. "Oh, look," I say dully. "Another promposal." Jackie half rises and cranes her neck, typing something furiously on her phone without looking. She takes a photo.

"What are you doing?"

"Writing an article about promposals." She sits back down. "Are you going to the prom?"

"Probably not."

"Why not?"

I sigh. "Ingrid and I were going to go together. Also, the only other people who have asked me to the prom have broken up with me or are not speaking to me. Also, prom seems silly."

"You're really not into high school traditions, are you?"

I sigh and look at the ceiling. "There's just not really much here for me anymore." Jackie has no response to that, and it occurs to me too late that what I said must have sounded incredibly sad. I ask, "Are you going?"

"Yeah. I'm the backup photographer. And I have to write about it for the paper. And, also, it's senior prom and that only happens once."

"Who's your date?"

"The eight people I'm fifth-wheeling." Jackie gives me a strained smile. "But it'll be fun."

Just then, my phone buzzes.

I scoop it up. It's a text from Max.

Max

Hey just got back from jk

Hk

Yeah let's hang out

I leap to heart-react to the message, not even caring that I might come off as desperate. Thank god Max is always circumnavigating the globe. Now I know the news hasn't made it to him yet. Finally, I have an in. I hold up my phone to Jackie. "We're going on a date."

Chapter Eighteen

"And this is the view from the top of Victoria Peak."

"That's *incredible*," I coo. I'm in a ridiculously expensive lounge set, draped over Max on his living room couch. It's just the two of us. Laurel's at some grueling Pilates class. The sunlight is making him sleepy. I'm trying not to throw up from anxiety and keep willing my muscles to relax. As if I could when a possible murderer is spooning me.

Max is flipping through his photos to try to fend off his jet lag, showing me shots of every possible detail of Hong Kong. Looking at the lush sloping green hills fusing with gleaming spires of the skyscrapers, the pictures of the street markets with steamed buns and piles of fruits, and the dazzling array of lights, I do feel an ugly twist of jealousy. I have distant family in Hong Kong, and yet my mom and I have never been able to afford a trip there. He gets to hop over there for a film festival without a second thought and act like he discovered the place.

"All I want is to re-create these *amazing* taro milk buns I had," Max says, looking them up on his phone. "You've had taro buns, right? It's, like, this creamy, sweet—"

I kiss him to make him stop explaining my culture to me. I need to wait for the right moment to start asking him about Ingrid. "Of course I have. I made my nanny buy them all the time."

"I want to go back next summer. Come with me? You could be my tour guide." He flips through a few more pictures. A shuffle of polished shoes filing into the subway. Weathered hands weighing oranges. A flash of someone at a table dimly lit by a neon blue light, head tilted back, tipping back a bottle of beer. "Central district was unreal. My boarding school buddy Jackson lives in HK now, so I got to go out with him. We were wiped by the end of that night."

He chuckles as a text flashes across the screen.

Do it now.

Max quickly swipes it away.

I bolt up. "What was that?"

"Oh, it's just this group chat I'm in," he says. "I have to tell my mom I'm not going to the Alps with her this summer. You wanna watch something? Let's watch something. I got really into *The Pitt* on the plane. Let's watch that."

He's talking really quickly, his voice rising in pitch. I remember the contact name: DB. Instantly—and I don't know why my brain latches onto this detail—I think back to Dalton being called *DB* by his friends at the debate tournament.

There's no way this is Dalton. They don't even know each other. I must be paranoid if I think it's him. I force myself to relax and settle back into Max. He slings an arm around me and snuggles me to him, but now it feels claustrophobic. "Sounds good."

The show we're watching becomes a blur of faces and escalating voices. I'm hyperaware of my breathing, of Max's arm tight around me. My hands feel cold.

Why did Ingrid call you?

How do I do this? How do I go about asking without tipping him off to what I know? Do I directly confront him? I think I have to; he's met all my previous attempts with lies or half-truths. And she called him. He knows her.

My voice quavers. "Um, this is kind of way back, but—"

Max snores loudly, startling me. I stare at him in disbelief. He must be beyond jet-lagged. His mouth is slightly open and he's drooling. I go to shake him, but my hand freezes midair. His phone, face up on the coffee table, keeps lighting up with texts.

There *is* a way to know without asking him. That is what I've learned: Phones reveal everything. I reach over and carefully pick up Max's cell. My hand is shaking, my palm slippery with sweat, but I keep a viselike grip. If I drop this phone, the opportunity is over.

Carefully, I hold it out over his face. Miraculously, the Face ID works. I stand quickly, cradling the phone to my chest. This is the moment of truth. I click on the chat and almost lurch backward. The names that texted were initials. And they were not talking about his mom. Max was lying. This group chat has three people in it. The two other people are DB and AK.

Suddenly, everything becomes so very apparent. I know beyond a shadow of a doubt that the group chat I'm staring at is with Aditya Kalra and Dalton Burke.

AK

You've gotta break up with her!

Max

But u guys just did it i can't do it without looking sus

Max

fuck me im stuck with her forever

DB

It is possible—just make up some bs reason about how you don't know if you can commit

Long distance, college, etc.

Do it now.

I sink to the floor, my hand clamped over my mouth.

They all *know each other.*

I was taking all these extra precautions to keep them apart. To make sure that none of them crossed paths. I thought I was orchestrating my three selves perfectly and that the only reason it all imploded is because of Jackie. But now I realize that *they've* been playing *me*, pretending to be the clueless, trusting boyfriends when all along, they've been in this group chat, discussing me. *For how long?*

I scroll up, before today, to this past weekend.

DB

Just ended things with her

AK

Same here thank GOD

Glad your debate friend pulled through. I was going to have to invite her to a family barbecue and have my dad's friend interrogate and expose her fake start-up

DB

That's a lot.

AK

I had to keep up the bit!! couldn't be the one to break up with her or she'd start suspecting me

DB

Had to invite her to my mom's art gala b/c my mom wanted to meet her, so i get it.

Max

gots to see it through

u got out tho

happy for u guys ugh

AK

You next bro

im stuck in Hong Kong pretending to not know a thing

also sloshed rn

does she suspect anything

AK

She doesn't

DB

not as of right now but keep us posted

How far does this go back? I'm no longer reading individual text messages. I'm scrolling frantically. The first message was on the day after Ingrid's candlelight vigil.

DB

The police came over to question me, FYI

Max

. . .

My parents hired lawyers. Got rid of the tape.

she just asked about your party though I played it cool

AK

We should be good right? There's no way to trace it back to us???

. . . unless the police hack into Ingrid's phone???

phone's in the ocean

DB

Police are ruling it an accident. Just saw on news

I'm staring at the chat, my eyes watering in horror, and it's all dawning on me. It wasn't just Max, like Jackie and I had thought. It was all three of them. Dalton, Aditya, Max—they all did it together. They *all* were responsible for Ingrid's death.

It takes me a moment to process the evidence in my hands. This confirms that they all killed my best friend. I try to move, but my body is frozen. My phone hovers right over Max's face. All this time I had been asking them about the specifics of Ingrid, grasping at any clues that could be of help to me and Jackie, and they've been lying to me. Playing clueless.

I need to get out of here. I slowly disentangle myself from him and grab my phone, too. He shifts a little and lets out a loud snore as I tiptoe across the ocean of a living room and then past the kitchen, past the rec room, past the workout room—why are there so many rooms in this house?—and ever so carefully pry open the door that leads to the backyard. The hinges squeak and I wince, but Max is still conked out.

I shut the door behind me and immediately call Jackie. It goes to voicemail. My heart is thrashing against the walls of my chest. Of course she responds immediately every other time, but I can't reach her this one time I need her. I text her, frantically:

Me

SOS I NEED YOU IM AT MAX BRACKENS HOUSE

HES IN A GROUP CHAT W DALTON AND ADITYA THEY ALL KILLED HER

TOGETHER

COME

DROPPING LOCATION

I stare hard at the phone screen, willing her to appear. But she doesn't respond. A small, panicked whimper escapes me. I'm on my own.

Okay, Amelia, focus! First, I'm going to take a screen recording of Max's phone. With shaking fingers, I go to the settings, turn the screen recording on, and scroll to the very top of the conversation. I scroll quickly. I need to be able to capture everything, but also, I'm racing against time. Max could sleep for five more seconds or five more hours. After what feels like an eternity, I'm at the start of the chat. As I move down the conversation, I feel more sick to my stomach—I piece together how everything went down. How Dalton had made the decision to leave her body there on the rocks at the bottom of the cliffs, knowing the high tide would take her out to sea. How Aditya had scoured the area to clean up any evidence that they were there and picked up the necklace that had broken in the scuffle. How they all went back to the party pretending nothing had happened, and Max created alibis for all of them to keep their stories straight. How it all went down after I'd left—after I'd offered to pick up Ingrid and she refused.

How they all wondered, after, if she was truly dead, or if there had been a possibility of saving her—but it was too late, and she was gone, swept out by the tide.

The red light pulses steadily in the upper right-hand corner. I keep scrolling and looking up to see if I'm alone. Finally, I reach today's conversation with all the urging to break up with me. I flick to Max's camera roll to find the screen recording. Among his recent photos are blurry pictures of him in Hong Kong and pictures of his ex-girlfriend. Has he been cheating on me this whole time? There's no time to think about that. I text myself the screen recording. The video file is massive and it takes forever to send, so I find myself scanning the colossal backyard. Around the grotesque apple Max's stepmom has finally installed in the background, I can see that the pool is still as glass. The backyard is surrounded by hedges. From this vantage point, it's a clear enough day to see to the ocean, down south to La Jolla. This is what Max saw the morning he came back from Dalton's party, after they killed Ingrid together and threw her body into the ocean. He probably sipped his coffee and looked out at this view, knowing that he would never get caught. And all this time, *they've* been pretending to date me, keeping the truth from me, outmaneuvering me. Dalton even said he loved me. Was that all for show? Did they pretend to be even *more* in love with me, have me meet their families, overdo the affection so I wouldn't suspect a thing? I get it now: They were protecting one another. The whole time they've all been living as murderers, and never once did they seem to care.

"So fucking depraved," I say aloud through gritted teeth.

From behind me, Max calls out, "*What?*"

I whirl around. Max is standing in the doorway. Slowly, he steps out and closes the door behind him. His cheeks are still pink from his nap, but his expression is alert, his eyes narrowed and focused solely on me. "Why are you holding my phone?"

Quickly, I shove his phone into my pocket. I look down and realize I've accidentally pocketed my *own* phone. His phone is still clutched tightly in my hand. Did the screen recording send? It went to sleep. I can't unlock it.

"Oh!" I laugh nervously. "My phone died, and I wanted to come outside . . . and take a picture. For my Stories, you know?"

Max shakes his head like he's talking to a toddler. "Okay, Amelia," he says very softly. "Let's just be real with each other."

The sound of my real name in his voice sends goose bumps up my arms. Max is still watching me intently. "Fine. What did you do to Ingrid? And why?"

"No. We're starting with you. What was your and Ingrid's plan?"

"What?"

"You acted like you were in love with me." Max sneers. "We were in a relationship. I thought it was real. And all this to discover that this whole time you were a relationship with two other people, lying about who you actually were."

I sniff. "Well, you were cheating on me with your ex, so you're one to talk. I saw your camera roll."

Max flings his hands out. "That's not even the fucking point! You lied about your entire identity, and I had to find out who you really are through a group chat!" His arms slap to his sides. "Do you know how insane it was for all of us to have to keep dating you and pretending to be *in love with you* and keep up this show? I mean, are you even an heiress? Did you grow up in Singapore? Was any of it true? Or was this all one lie after another? You were actually scamming people for fun?"

Max is blocking the doorway and my only way out. I'm

terrified. Still, I smile dangerously. “And if I was? What, girls can’t have hobbies?”

“You’re sick in the head,” Max rants. “Both of you. She came up with the idea, and then what, deployed you to ruin our lives?”

“You killed her!” I shriek at him. “You and Dalton and Aditya—you killed her together.”

Max steps toward me. “Don’t say that.”

I completely underestimated him. Him, his family, Bracken Pharma—all of it has always been a threat.

“You did, didn’t you?” My heart is racing. My limbs feel loose and confused, and I’m delirious with fear. I stumble toward him. “You killed her, and then you all kept dating me so I wouldn’t get suspicious. Tell me. What did you do that night, Max? What happened at the party? How did you kill her?”

“Keep your voice down,” Max says through gritted teeth.

“Don’t deny it!” Tears spring to my eyes. “I read your group chat, you know. It’s all on there. You killed her. You killed her with your bare hands and then you went on like nothing ever happened!”

“I didn’t mean to!” Max crumples, sinking to the grass, and he’s letting out these braying noises that I think is crying. “All we wanted from Ingrid was the truth. I was just trying to get it out of her. I didn’t mean to push her.”

Something is buzzing in my pocket. *Jackie!* I place my hand in my pocket and swipe my thumb across the screen, praying I’ve answered the call and not declined it. I step closer.

“You pushed her?” I ask, my voice wavering. “Over that cliff?”

“She met us on the cliffs on that trail outside of Dalton’s house,” Max says through sobs. “But we were all drunk, and it was dark, and we couldn't see anything. I think she was especially drunk, and she was stumbling, and she was just getting madder and madder at us, and then—" He hiccups.

"And then what?" I whisper, feeling like I am having an out-of-body experience. I am in the home of a killer who is crying. Once, he was scared of a grasshopper in his own house, and he made me carry it out and release it in the garden in a cup. And yet he murdered my best friend.

"She just—fell." His voice cracks at the last word. "She lost her balance and then she fell, and then we didn't realize that it was an actual cliff until we heard her hit the rocks below." His face contorts to an open-mouthed grimace.

"She fell because you pushed her," I croak.

"We were all drunk," he repeats. "I didn't mean it. I didn't even push her that hard." He looks up at me, and his eyes are red-rimmed.

"But you still pushed her!" I shriek. "And you saw her fall, and you didn't do anything. You didn't call for help. You let her die. You dumped her in the *ocean*."

"Stop." Max is clutching his head in his hands. "None of this would have happened if you'd just left me alone!"

My head is spinning. I need to get out of here. "Fine." I stand up. "I will, then."

"Wait." Max pushes himself to his feet, swiping at his cheeks. "Where are you going?"

"I'm going home."

"No. You can't."

"What do you mean, I can't?" I snap. "You're just going to keep me hostage here?"

"Give me my phone. Now!"

I jump at his raised voice. It's useless to me if I can't unlock it, so I toss it to the grass. He doesn't reach for it, just looks at it.

"Now give me your phone," Max demands.

He's still between me and the sliding glass door back into the kitchen, which is my only way out of here. I clutch my phone to my chest. The screen is black, and my stomach drops—I must have declined Jackie's call. No one is coming to help me. And I know Max wants to keep me here, or hurt me, or silence me.

"I'm not going to do anything," I lie, trying to placate him. "Come on. We can let all of this go. I'm going to keep this between us, okay? Please just let me go home."

Max doesn't budge. "And why should I ever believe you?"

I open my mouth but it's like my vocal cords are frozen. I don't know if it's the angle of the sun, or the change of the light, but he has this strange, glazed, off-kilter look in his eyes.

"You shouldn't have gone through my phone," Max continues. "It was better that you didn't know."

Hurriedly, I scan the massive yard. There's an opening in the hedges that I could push through, end up in the neighbor's yard, maybe. I could try to lure him away and run into the house, which is my best shot of getting to my car keys. He's certainly not letting me walk free.

Hedges or door. I can only pick one place to run toward.

I pick hedges.

Chapter Nineteen

This yard is so impossibly large. Max chases after me, screaming at me to stop. As I get closer to the hedges, I realize that behind them is a ten-foot wrought-iron fence. There's no way to squeeze through or climb up.

Heart pounding, I glance backward. Max has almost caught up to me. I whirl around.

"You want to get me, huh?" I taunt, secretly panicked.

He's spent years playing rugby. He's brought boys twice my size down in a tackle. And now my back is against the hedges and I'm trapped. Still, I wait until he's close enough to me. Then I do the only thing I can think of: I hurl my phone at his face.

"Agh!" he screams. His hands fly up and I'm sprinting at an angle, away from him. I weave through the pool chairs. Max is staggering behind, his hand clutching his right eye. He lunges forward and wildly grabs at me. I dodge him, putting distance between us, upending the pool chairs, trying to slow down his advance in any way.

"Stop fucking up Laurel's Scandinavian pool chairs!" he screeches.

I heave another one for good measure.

I'm in the clear. All I have to do is make it to the sliding glass door, and I can slam it and lock him out. I risk a look back. He's clambering over a pool chair. A little farther and then—

My foot catches on something and my head slams into solid metal.

I recoil and crumple to the ground. When I come to, I'm seeing double. My head is throbbing and the world is spinning. I'm looking up at that big ugly metallic apple sculpture that his stepmom ordered. It looms over me. There's nothing I can do but scream.

A hand instantly clamps over my mouth.

"Shut up!" Max hisses.

I kick out but my feet only connect with air. Waves of dizziness crash into me and I feel like I'm going to throw up. There are two Maxes. Two apples. Disoriented, I try to push him away, but he has a strong grip on me now, one hand still shoved over my mouth. Everything hurts. I bite down until I taste blood. Max shrieks in pain, rips his hand from my mouth, and then grapples me in a headlock, cutting off my air.

God, I used to love those strong arms. Now they're trying to kill me. Flailing, I try to hit, scratch, kick, anything. But my eyes are going to burst out of my head. I can't see straight. I can hear my pulse thrum in my ears. I kick and my knees scrape concrete and I shout out, or try to, at least, and Max slams my head to the ground.

There is only sky and trees. It's as if my memories have scattered like marbles. All I can think of is Ingrid. Her smiling at me as she looks back from the cliff. Us sleeping, facing each other, unable to part even for hours. How could I ever let her go? The memory of her is too strong.

Dimly, I smell chlorine. At once, I understand where Max is dragging me to—the pool. I claw for purchase but the concrete scrapes my fingers raw.

"This is what you get for choosing to mess with me."

He's going to hold me down in his pool and drown me. He's going to load my body into one of his ten Teslas and drive to the marina, and then he's going to put me in his sailboat and dump my body into the ocean until I sink, until my body bloats and I return to the shore, broken and dripping and gray, just like Ingrid.

All because of *that bronze apple*.

I thrash but the force is too strong. He pushes my head into the pool water. The freezing cold is a shock, and I gasp as a reflex. I remember that I should be trying to conserve my breath, but it's too late—I've gulped down water, and I'm trying to cough it out but there's nothing but chlorinated water flooding my mouth and nose, forcing its way into my throat and choking me. I know I'm done for.

Was this what Ingrid felt in her last moments, too?

Suddenly, the pressure on my head eases.

Someone drags me up by my shirt and I flop onto the concrete, gagging and coughing. I can only turn and vomit up water. I convulse into a fetal position, still coughing violently, sucking in air.

"Amelia!" I hear someone scream, and realize it's a girl's voice. Someone hits me on the back and I vomit up more water.

"Amelia, oh my god, you're alive. I thought it was too late."

My lungs feel raw. I look up blearily at the person who saved me. Slowly the world comes back into focus.

"Jackie?" I try to croak, but my throat isn't working right now. I just cough.

She's holding a glass bottle in her hands, and I realize it's a heavy water jug. She drops it.

"My god," she murmurs, "you're okay."

I'm shivering. She pulls me to her and grabs my face in her hands, touching her forehead to mine. Her cheeks are red and blotchy and she's sobbing.

"You're okay." She cries, relieved.

Max is lying on the grass. He groans and stirs, so Jackie whacks his head once more for good measure. He goes still.

We both look at him for a second.

"Is he—" I cough more. "Did you—"

"Just knocked him out," Jackie says. "I think."

Jackie works fast. She takes off her sweater and ties it around his hands. By the time Max is moving again, he's squirming on his stomach and his hands are tied behind his back.

My teeth are chattering and I'm still shivering violently. "We need to call—"

"Already did. They're on the way." Jackie wipes the water from my face with her sleeve and drapes her jean jacket over my shoulders. She looks at me and sniffles. "Are you sure you're okay?"

"I know. I look terrible."

Jackie scans my body. Her gaze lands on my scraped knee.

It looks ugly. "I was so scared for you. We need to get you to the hospital."

"No, I'm—" I double over and vomit more water, and then something else. I think it's remnants of my lunch.

"Yeah. You need a checkup." Jackie kneels in front of me. Two Jackies. They weave in and out of each other.

I blink. "How did you get here?"

"I missed your first call," Jackie admits. "But then I called again, and you answered. So the whole time you were talking to Max, I could hear everything." She pauses. "Don't worry. I have the evidence. I recorded the entire conversation."

I sag in relief. "Oh my god, Jackie. I could kiss you right now."

"Okay. I think you're concussed or something." She laughs uneasily. "But yeah. I think halfway through the call I knew you were in danger, so I looked up Max's address on the internet and came here. And I saw him . . ." Her face scrunches and she shakes her head.

"I know," I croak. "It was a close call."

"He killed Ingrid. He was going to kill you, too."

"But he won't," I tell her. "Because of you. You saved me, Jackie. And he won't get away with it this time."

As if summoned, Max starts groaning. Jackie pins him down. Finally, we hear sirens in the distance.

Chapter Twenty

The police and the ambulance pull up to the Bracken compound at the same time. The police take Max away and demand that Jackie go with them to the precinct. I want to go, too, but Jackie tells them what happened and the paramedics tell me I need medical attention now. They take me to the hospital. They run a series of tests and scans, and they determine that I'm badly concussed. Jackie's right. She always is. My lungs have mostly expelled all the water but they still run chest X-rays just in case there's fluid buildup. My leg is bleeding profusely, but it seems to be just a scrape. I won't even need stitches.

When my mother rushes in and asks me what happened, I just tell her it was a bad date. A really bad one. I'll explain more to her later when I can think straight. Literally.

They determine that my concussion is pretty gnarly, so they monitor me overnight. Whether it was from me crashing into Laurel's apple sculpture or from Max bashing my head to the concrete is to be determined. Jackie returns from the precinct. She's turned over to them the recording of my conversation with Max. She told them that she broke into Max's house to see him trying to kill me. She's shaking when she tells me this. She's traumatized. I mean, I think I'm traumatized, too, but my damaged brain is taking a minute to process everything. Everything just feels too confusing and bright. It's a relief to lie back down and close my eyes.

Mom takes the day off work and just sits with me at the hospital. I tell her that it's okay, that they're just monitoring me as a precaution, but she stays by my side and doesn't leave. The next day, they discharge me from the hospital and she drives me home, where I rest for three days and see no one. The police want to talk to me, but I'm in no shape to even go outside, let alone recount in detail what happened to me.

I stay home from school. I'm told to stay away from screens. My mom takes another whole week off work to care for me. She keeps asking me what happened; the police only told her bits and pieces. My mind grasps at details to pull together and what to omit from the story. My mother's poor heart can only take so much. Instead, I stay quiet, saying it hurts to talk.

The only person I speak to is Jackie, late at night, under my blankets to muffle the sound. She tells me that Max has been arrested, as have Dalton and Aditya, based on her recording. But they've all got lawyers and they're refusing to talk. Everyone is waiting for my statement.

"I can't tell the truth," I say to her, my eyes closed to stop the spinning. It's calming, looking into nothingness. "I never thought about this. If this starts getting out on national news, in the media, everywhere—"

"Let's just see how this all plays out, okay?" Jackie interrupts. "I actually think you'll be fine if this leaks. I mean, aren't scammers kind of having a moment right now?" She laughs wryly. "Maybe you'll end up on *Dancing with the Stars*. Besides, even if you don't reveal your real reason, scamming billionaires' sons is kind of funny. I feel like you'd be more popular than you think."

"But Bracken can't know I'm looking into them," I tell her. "Ingrid tried to and Max *killed* her for that. He would have killed me. If I reveal what Bracken has done, think of what they could do to me."

Jackie is silent over the line for a moment. "Surely they can't do anything to you," she finally says. But even she sounds doubtful.

"They're pharmaceutical billionaires. They can do anything." My chest feels like it's constricting. "And at the very least, if the truth comes out, their lawyers and families will say I ruined lives. They'll call me a slut. They'll ruin my image. Ingrid's, too."

Who cares if we had good intentions? Who cares if Aditya's family is short five grand of seed funding that he would have given to an evil surveillance start-up that mass-produced killing drones? Who cares if I stole from Celia Burke's congressional campaign?

"My life is at risk," I argue. "And my reputation." And Ingrid's. I can't take her reputation down with mine.

"That's true," Jackie agrees, but her voice sounds reluctant. She pauses. "Well, in that case, sounds like we need to make up a convincing story."

My mom goes back to doing half shifts. I rest at home. After another whole week, I find that one day, I can stand up without severe pain and nausea. My mom drives me to the police station where I provide my statement. I tell them about the night of Dalton's party.

I tell them about how I briefly talked to the boys in one of the upstairs rooms, how Max flirted with me and then made a disparaging comment about my body when I turned him down; after all, I was already dating Aditya. That's what Jackie told me to say. I tell them that Ingrid passed the room and saw me upset. I tell them that I ran out of the party and left, but Ingrid must have stayed. Must have followed the boys to the cliffs, where they were hanging out, all drunk and high. She yelled at them; Max got aggressive and shoved her and Ingrid slipped from the cliff's edge. Dalton and Aditya helped Max push her body out to sea. *She was a good friend*, I say. *She was just trying to protect me, like always.*

After that night, I tell the police, I broke up with Aditya for not coming to my defense. Max felt so guilty that he called me to apologize for making that comment and asked me on a date so he could keep tabs on me. When I was hanging out with him, I found all the texts on his phone. The texts about him, Dalton, and Aditya covering up Ingrid's murder.

This is a version of the story that lines up with Jackie's recording of my conversation with Max. This is the story that I can bear to tell my mother. The evidence is on my side—my screen recording of their group chat didn't send because the file was too large. The boys won't talk, either, won't contest this story because of their lawyers.

Ingrid's family comes over and brings me food. They fuss over me and bring Neosporin for my scrapes and also a neck pillow they bought that they say helps with concussion recovery. They thank me for bringing justice to Ingrid, and they're crying so hard, they can barely form those words. I cry because this won't bring back Ingrid, and we know it, but maybe this will all give us a little more closure. We know what happened. After they leave, I lie on the couch in the dark room, my eyes closed. I replay those horrific moments at Max's pool, and I feel a little queasy again, and then my mind thankfully blocks it out. I can't tell if it's the bruised brain or the PTSD kicking in, trying to protect me.

Jackie visits me one night when my mom is at work and back to full night shifts. She looks at me, then raises an eyebrow. "Prada sunglasses?"

"These were the only sunglasses I could find," I protest. They were Laurel's.

Jackie shakes her head and holds up a bag. "I brought you dinner. Grain bowl with salmon, salad, nuts. They're all supposed to be good for concussion recovery."

I'm touched by how thoughtful this is. "Oh, wow. You really did your research."

"Well, I figured this was the first day your mom went back to work, so I'd come make sure you're fed. I got myself the same." She surveys her surroundings.

"Sorry, it's not that big in here," I say. "It's just me and my mom." I think of Jackie's polished house, with the neat slabs and sharp angles, and feel self-conscious.

"No, I like it," Jackie replies earnestly. "It's very cozy."

We eat together. I put on those mindless HGTV shows my mom likes to watch, but it's really just background noise because I still can't look at screens. The salmon bowl is so good, but maybe just because I've been ravenous and haven't really had much food all day. I'm pretty sure I look like shit in my second-day pajamas and just-showered hair. But Jackie doesn't comment on it. She talks and talks, and that's exactly what I need right now. She tells me newspaper room drama about how two girls wanted the same guy to ask them out. She tells me about how a kid almost started a school fire in the chem lab the other day and everyone had to evacuate and some people just ditched and went to the beach. And, of course, she tells me about the ongoing criminal case with the three boys.

Most of this I already know. Aditya and Dalton got arrested the day after Max was. Naturally, they immediately came armed with legal representation, so thankfully not much is coming from them in the way of statements, which helps with the story I told the police. But the gossip, Jackie informs me, is wild. Three golden boys from quiet San Diego, wrapped up in a potential murder case.

"I've seen social media posts about it. It was even mentioned on *Beyond Reasonable Doubt* the other day."

"They're already talking about this on true crime podcasts?"

"A passing mention, but yes."

"Is the story holding up?"

"So far, yes. The boys aren't talking. They're sticking to your side of the story."

I slump back in relief. "Good."

"I figured they would. It makes it look like an accident, not a premeditated attack to cover up Bracken's crimes." Jackie pauses. "Oh, I got you out of that *Macbeth* project, by the way. I told Mr. Aguilar I'd take it on."

"Really?"

"Yeah." Jackie shrugs. "I told him about your condition in detail, and he felt bad for you. You're excused from any AP Lang homework for the rest of the year. Besides, I knew you didn't read the play, anyway."

I roll my eyes behind my sunglasses and hope she can't see it. But mostly, I'm just grateful and relieved, and though I'm too prideful to admit it, I give a suppressed smile and hope Jackie knows just how much that means to me.

"Okay, I should go." Jackie stands up and brushes crumbs off her jeans.

"Thanks for dinner," I say. "That was really nice of you."

"I'll be back tomorrow with another salmon grain bowl."

No one's ever cared for me like this before. Not even Ingrid. How did I overlook how kind she is, how thoughtful? I walk her to the door of my apartment. Right before she goes down the stairs, I call out, "Hey, Jackie."

She looks back.

I shift from my right foot to my left. "Do you, um, want to go to the prom with me?"

Jackie nearly loses her balance. "What?"

I repeat, louder, "Do you—"

"No, I heard what you said." She stops short. "You're asking me to the prom? As . . . a date?"

"Yeah. I am."

"This is the head wound, isn't it?" She nervously laughs. "You've hit your head, and now you're seeing double, or you're playing a joke on me—"

"I'm serious," I insist. "Would it really be so strange? I know we used to hate each other, and we will still probably annoy the hell out of each other, but you also really get me and, you know, I actually think we'd have a lot of fun together."

Finally, Jackie's eyes widen. Her expression softens. The corner of her mouth tilts up until this incredulous smile flutters across her face—a beautiful, hopeful, elusive smile I somehow want to keep chasing. "You're serious?"

I nod and smile back. "I know this isn't the best way of asking. But, you know, limited brain capacity."

"Of course, Amelia," she says. "I'll absolutely go to the prom with you."

Chapter Twenty-One

The day the boys get arraigned in court, I go to Ingrid's house to have dinner with her parents.

"That Bracken kid was charged with involuntary manslaughter, aggravated assault, and concealment," Ingrid's dad reads off his phone screen. "Other two charged with concealment of an accidental death. They all pled not guilty. Thankfully, they're all eighteen, so they're getting tried in the adult criminal system."

"They should have been charged with more," Ingrid's mom says. She grips the serving fork so tightly that her knuckles are white. "That's too light for them."

"They hired the best defense."

"Of course they did. But they dumped Ingrid's body in the ocean." Her voice rises. "They tried to kill Amelia when she found out. I mean, look at what they did to you." She waves her hands at me. "They nearly cracked your skull open."

I blink. I know I look like shit right now.

"Sorry, sweetie. I'm just saying, I want to kill those boys for hurting you like this." She serves me a heaping plate of garlic herb potatoes, which smell incredible. Her parents are finally cooking again. "Honey, what did Max say to you at that party that started all this?"

I swallow hard and my throat bobs.

"She doesn't need to explain it," Ingrid's dad quickly says. "We don't need to know."

"Ingrid should have never been at that party!" Ingrid's mom cries.

Silence falls across the room. Ingrid's dad looks at his plate.

I watch as Ingrid's mom shrinks back. "Sorry," she says again. "I just . . . I've just been having these . . . outbursts lately. I've been working through it with my grief therapist." Her expression contorts. "I'm just having a hard time accepting this."

"I'm so sorry," I whisper. "It was my fault. She was defending me."

"No. *No.*" Ingrid's mom leans forward. "Those boys are dangerous. With the positive toxicology report, we're thinking they drugged her, too. That should be all over the news, but it's not." She stabs her potatoes. "We don't need to keep talking about this. Come on, let's eat."

I hate that I'm lying to Ingrid's parents. *But this will protect them*, I tell myself. This keeps Ingrid's reputation in the clear, too. Standing up for me in her last moments.

Here's what I'm *not* allowed to tell Ingrid's parents: Last weekend, while my mom was at work, the day before I went to the police station to give my statement, a lawyer came to my apartment to meet with me. He had close-set dark brown eyes, gelled curls, and a watch that gleamed. He was in a crisp, tailored navy suit, and when he handed me his business card at the door, I picked it up and knew immediately that I was looking at the biggest threat to my life right now. I let him in and we sat at the dining table.

"Emmanuel Auguste," he said simply, by way of introduction.

"I'm a representative of Maximilian Bracken's family. Thank you for meeting with me, Amelia."

I nodded, staring at the files in front of him through my sunglasses.

"Let's look at the situation we have on hand here. Would you care to take me through the details of your defrauding of the Bracken family, the Burke family, and the Kalra family?"

My eyes snapped up from the file to his.

"It is my understanding that you and Ingrid Mitchell knowingly conspired to deceive and defraud these families under false identities," Emmanuel continued. "The Kalra family is thinking about suing you. The Burke family is accusing you of siphoning stolen campaign funds."

My mouth felt dry and I forced myself to swallow. I was glad he couldn't see my expression. "I don't know what you mean," I said, trying to stay calm. "I don't need to talk to you."

Emmanuel nodded. "Of course, you're right, and I appreciate the courtesy of this conversation. Let me make this more succinct. There are two ways we can tell the story. I think you can understand this analogy, given your narrative . . . strengths. The first version of the story is that there is a possibility of a voluntary manslaughter charge, but there would be a lengthy court process. Sure, Max accidentally pushed Ingrid off those cliffs, but he only did so because he was so distraught by malicious deceit and manipulation *planned* by you and Ingrid. He can be tried and determined guilty by the court, but you, too, could be brought up on criminal charges. And the reputational damage to both of your lives, your families, would be . . . irreversible."

My breath solidified in my chest. I immediately thought of

Ingrid's parents finding out, of my mother knowing the truth. It terrified me.

"Or," Emmanuel interjected, "there's another version of the truth we can tell based on the evidence we have. One that circumvents the need to take this to court."

He slid across a sheet of paper.

"What if things got out of hand at this party? You never know what reckless things teenagers might do. So one could easily surmise that they had too much to drink and did a few party drugs and then they just went for a walk. They were rowdy and horsing around, and, of course, the cliffs were unstable, so Ingrid just . . . fell. Their crime is that they were reckless, and negligent in getting Ingrid the care she needed. Involuntary manslaughter." He leans back. "Do you see what I'm saying, Amelia?"

I skimmed the sheet of paper in front of me. "Is this an NDA?"

"A generous one," Emmanuel said. "We're working on a plea deal right now that depends on the statement you make. This version of events is very believable to me. But it needs your cooperation, too. Sign, and your and Ingrid's reputations remain intact. Your deception will stay between us." He flipped the page, and with his other hand he slid over a check with a number that made me even dizzier. "And, of course, I need to mention . . . Mr. Peter Bracken hoped to make your decision slightly more intuitive. If you sign, you will receive a payout that will cover all future college expenses. For all the trouble."

I looked at the check, which was a life-changing amount of money, and then at the NDA. The words swam in front of me. What else could I do? I picked up the pen and signed on the dotted line. That night, I got on the phone with Jackie and we made up our story for the police. I just didn't tell her the part about the lawyer. I don't want Jackie in danger, too.

Now, at Ingrid's house, I'm helping clear the dishes to the sink.

Mrs. Mitchell says, "I was thinking of setting up some kind of fund in her memory, like to make a scholarship in her name or something. We had all this money we saved for her college. We want it to go to someone."

I turn to her. "I think that's a beautiful idea. And people would donate, too."

"You think?"

"Just look at how many people showed up at her vigil." My voice breaks. "She was so loved."

"She was, wasn't she?" Ingrid's mother hunches over the sink. When she's done rinsing the dishes, she wipes her hands on the towel and gives me a hug. "Thank you for being here," she whispers into my shoulder. "Thank you for what you did for her. You were—are—like family to us. You know that?"

"Max charged with aggravated assault for you and involuntary manslaughter and concealment of an accidental death for Ingrid." Jackie scrolls through her phone in the passenger seat of my car. "Aditya and Dalton charged with the concealment of an accidental death. Pled not guilty for now, but seems like lawyers could be going for a plea deal."

"I saw."

"The story worked."

I nod. "Thank god," I say, but Jackie's frowning. "What's up?"

She sighs through gritted teeth. "Do you think . . . this is all over?"

"What do you mean?"

"I mean, I can't believe Bracken just got away with that." She shakes her head. "Such a light charge. I mean, they're really murderers. Someone should bring them down."

"I tried," I say tiredly. "I really did. This story protects me. Ingrid, too."

"I know," Jackie says. "What an evil corporation."

I'm starting to feel sick again. Maybe this concussion isn't done yet. "I just . . . maybe this is something we let go for now. I don't know if I have the capacity for this." I lean my head against her shoulder and whisper, "It gives me nightmares."

I'm aware of how plaintive and vulnerable I sound. But I can be this raw around Jackie and it's a relief. Jackie simply puts her arm around me and pulls me in for a hug. "I'm sorry. Let's talk about something else."

"It's okay. I'm hungry. Can we eat now?"

This time, we've picked up pizzas from Isola. They have a Thursday deal where it's two pizzas for twenty dollars. It's become our thing. Every week, we pick up something and walk along the beach. Jackie always brings beverages. She has Diet Coke this time. I contribute chocolate chip cookies I made with Ingrid's recipe. She makes a little spread on the beach. It's nowhere near the picnics I used to have, back when I'd wear a full face of makeup, back when I'd preen and worry about which version of myself to become. My face is bare. When I eat my pizza slices they fold and the sauce runs and toppings fall off and I make a mess, but there's no way not to. I look terrible, and yet when Jackie glances my way, she beams.

We watch the sun set, talk about our future, about Northern California, about Ingrid. Jackie rambles about the various ways to potentially hack into Bracken. She tells me about this book she read, about this start-up in Silicon Valley that was almost valued at a billion dollars until someone in the company discovered that it was all fake. I just watch her talk. I think I'm staring at her too much because suddenly she stops. "What?"

Her brown eyes look like amber in the sunlight, and suddenly I want to memorize every detail of her face. How did I not see any of this before? How determined she can be. How much she is willing to go to the ends of the earth for someone she cares about. I am awash with affection, something I've only had a hint of before, but now I decide, in this moment, that I'm going to act on it. I keep staring at her.

"You have a bit of pizza sauce at the corner of your mouth." I reach out, brush her lips with my fingertips, but I don't withdraw my hand. She realizes it at the same time I do. Her eyes meet mine, and when I draw in, they close. I'm breathing hard. My heart's fluttering in my chest.

"I have pizza breath," she warns.

"I don't care."

My lips brush hers, softly at first. She tastes sweet, like soda. And then she pulls me by my shirt, kissing me deeper, until our hands are tangled in each other's hair, until I lose sense of the world around me.

It is, surprisingly and unsurprisingly, the most perfect kiss I've ever experienced in my life.

Chapter Twenty-Two

Neither of us really cares about prom, which almost makes it more fun. The week before the big day, Jackie and I go thrifting in Mira Mesa for dresses. I find a pastel blue chiffon dress that flounces out and drapes over my tall frame. When Jackie steps out of the changing room with a deep emerald green, form-fitting dress that makes my jaw drop, I reach over and kiss her for all the Goodwill security cameras to see.

And prom, when it does come, is surprisingly so fun.

I can't tell if people are more surprised by my return or by the fact that Jackie and I are together. We go with a group of Jackie's newspaper friends. We clamber into someone's giant house and take pictures. We do limoncello shots until we're giggly. We leave and get sushi, all of us, and someone is dared to eat a huge ball of wasabi, but it's so intense, he has to spit it out. When the bill comes, we all look around at one another nervously until I finally slide over my card as a gesture of chivalry. And then we all Uber to prom, and by the time we get there, we're drunk and having the best time of our lives.

Cramming into the photo booth with ten people. Fighting with classmates for access to the chocolate fountain. Flashing our song requests up to the DJ. This is what high school could have been like, I realize. School dances are fun. I never had to miss out on any of it.

Jackie disappears for a while because that overachiever is also on the school photography committee and she has to run around taking pictures. But when the slow dance song comes, I look across the room and she's there. Smiling, she shrugs off the camera and makes her way over to me. It's almost like the crowd parts for her. She reaches me, and I take her in my arms, and we come together, Jackie's head against my chest. When the song is done she looks at me, and at the same time, we lean in for a kiss.

When we part, the swirling light is shining on her. She looks up at me with her doe eyes and I picture us curled up next to each other at the beach and sneaking in makeouts, going on dates, being together for a summer. I thought I was done with relationships. It surprises me how much I want this one—this time for real.

I wake to the early light filtering through Jackie's curtains. My mouth is sticky and dry; my eyes burn from my dried-out contacts that I forgot to take out last night. My hair is crunchy from hairspray and I'm pretty sure I'm emitting glitter from all my pores. I disentangle myself from Jackie, who's sleeping curled up on her side, her cropped hair splayed on the pillow. She looks so sweet in her sleep, and suddenly I'm filled with affection and a protectiveness over her. I kiss her along the curve of her jaw and she barely stirs. Then I think about last night and my face gets hot. I want to curl up next to her warmth and sink back into sleep. But part of me is clammy and anxious, the gathering signs of a hangover. Water and a walk will fix it.

I carefully pick up our prom dresses, which have been tangled in a heap on the floor, and fold them over her desk chair. Then I pick out a T-shirt and a pair of cutoff jean shorts from the bottom of her closet and I throw them on. I peek downstairs; her mom's car isn't in the driveway, which is a relief. She must have gone to a workout class. I didn't want to confront Ms. Tran on a post-prom walk of shame. I grab a bottle of water from the pantry and slip out the door, closing it behind me. I text Jackie: **on a walk. Be back soon.**

My body knows exactly where it's taking me, even before my mind registers. I amble along the sloping sidewalks until I get to the cliffs that overlook the La Jolla Shores Beach Club.

It's early; in a few hours I know the sidewalks will be full of tourists descending upon the beach. But for now, it's just me and the rocks and the expanse of the sea. I follow the path down the sandy cliffs, and I am careful. So careful. I know how high the cliffs are now. How easy it is to slip, fall, crash into the rocks below and be swallowed by the gaping waves.

From this vantage point I see everything—the blues of the sky seeping into the ocean until they've become one; the tinges of the softest pink and the lightest brush of the clouds; I can smell the brine of the ocean fermenting in the air. The palm fronds waving. I can see below where the seals are nipping at each other before they heave themselves on the rocks for another day in the sun.

And across the cove, far below and nestled between the rocks, I can see the pristine stretch of white sand; the place where Ingrid and I reinvented ourselves. And for that moment, I look at the cliffs and imagine I'm talking to my best friend.

Part Three

The Truth

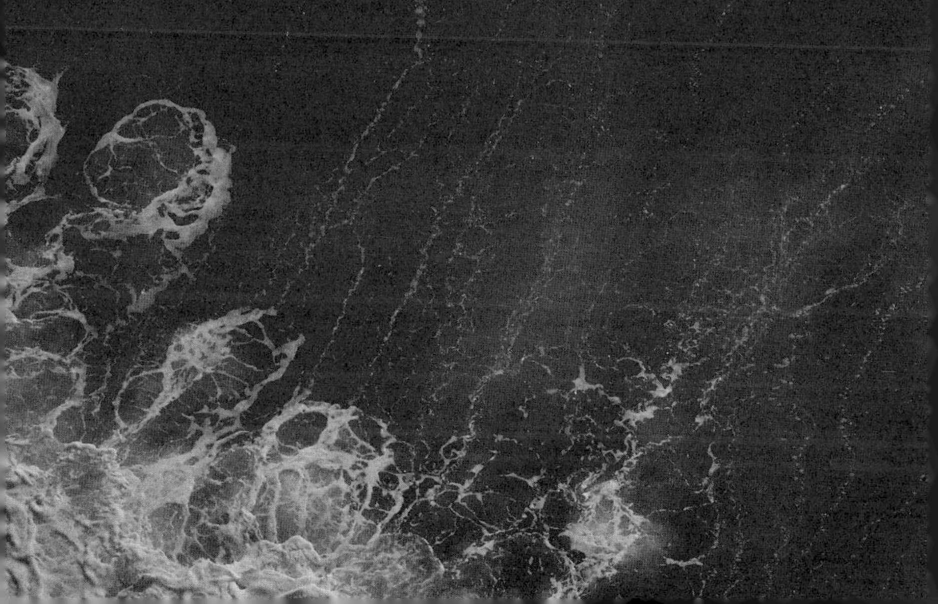

Chapter Twenty-Three

It was just an innocuous scroll; isn't that how it all starts? We all do it. We catch someone's Stories on social media, look at their profile, and before we know it, we're twenty posts deep, three years ago, praying that we don't like something by accident. It was a summer whim. A curiosity that simmered into infatuation, slow enough that we didn't even realize it at first. Your infatuation with Dalton was so apparent from the moment he walked through the La Jolla Shores Beach Club doors that summer before senior year, when you'd visit me at my job after your internship. How I felt when you talked about him, and how I wished—so badly, I remember—that you would stop longing for him, because it was evident the pain it gave you, to see someone that you knew for a fleeting summer who would now barely give you a passing look. I wanted things to go back to how they were, even though I didn't know exactly what that baseline was, when things were good and normal. I just remembered you happy before, Ingrid. I wanted that for you.

I was working at the La Jolla Shores Beach Club restaurant part-time after spending mornings in an internship where I froze my ass off through my layered cardigan in a UC San Diego lab. The beach club job was kind of demeaning—why did people care so much about making me move their chair two inches to the right, or about the plating, or sending a drink back and demanding I regarnish with a better slice of pineapple? But the pay was okay and the tips, at least, were decent. And it was fun with you. You came at first because I'd get you free virgin piña coladas. We'd eavesdrop on people's ridiculous conversations, pretend that we, too, had companies that just IPO'd, or that we weren't invited to our second cousin's wedding at an Italian villa. We'd hear full names and look them up on the internet. And then you saw Dalton Burke walk in with his parents, warm you with the heat of his smile, apologize for them fighting and taking it out on the poor boy setting up the beach umbrella, and then, suddenly, a crush from debate summer camp had been revived and he became the main character in the stories we told about each other. "He kissed me at debate camp," you'd said, leaning on the counter on your elbows, resting your cheek on your forearm. "Just once, on this walk through the University of Michigan Law Quad." You'd tilted your phone screen toward me, awash with pictures of their family trip to Costa Rica, tanned in the surf, his dark hair lightened slightly by the sun, zooming in on pictures of previous girlfriends in their sweaters and linen shorts, nails perfect, hair highlighted, speculating on what it would be like to date him.

Who could blame you? It was clear, the magnitude of the crush you had. The way you found excuses to now come to the beach club all the time, to linger—to strain to overhear his conversations and butt in, to talk to me loudly about this history book you were reading just on the off chance he would hear. It was transparent, all of it, especially to me, because I knew you and I knew your desperation, how badly you wanted to be liked.

And apparently, he could tell, too, because when he was hanging out with a friend one day and they looked in our direction, the wind carried their voices enough to overhear: "I think she's into you." We heard Dalton respond, "I know. She's obvious as fuck, I don't know how to tell her it's cringe." And I saw your face fall. Mine did, too, at the callousness, the flippancy with which he said it.

And I comforted you in my car that day, as you joked, snotty-nosed, "You should date him and ruin his life."

Your words. We plotted it on the way to your house for a sleepover, took a walk and split a joint that you stole from one of your theater friends, and, giggling and leaning into each other on the cliffs overlooking the ocean, amalgamated all evidence of Dalton's previous girlfriends and interests, and created the girl of his dreams.

Amy Fang was your idea. The things he liked—the kinds of snacks, the kinds of books he read, the girls you saw him date at camp—you tried that all on me to curate the perfect, ruthless revenge. I would date him, string him along, make him fall in love with me, and then break up with him in a devastating way to hurt him the way he'd hurt you. What a brilliant idea it all was. I hate that you tried to make me take credit.

And you encouraged me. You egged me on. Talked about how funny it would be as a bit, taking his ego down a notch. Brainstormed photo shoots, outfits, playlists, stories with me. You wanted to have him, in a way, with me as a proxy. When you talked about Bracken Pharma's annoying CEO's son who was in your internship program and stole credit for your work—and this was weeks before your mom got laid off during the summer—in a fit of rage, we added Max Bracken to our revenge list, scouring his public profile (of course his was public for his nonexistent film résumé) and crafting Mia Leung, his dazzling muse.

Although, I do have to say, Aditya was mine. We used to be in tennis classes together. We were paired up for drills and practice games, and I beat him every time. He didn't remember me, either, the first time he showed up at the La Jolla Shores Beach Club. Now I was the one who was looking up his profile, his stats, and realizing that the kid who was once scared of an errant flying tennis ball was now a prodigy. Him I dated because I wanted to, because I knew that I could never date him in real life, that I would never match up, and so I became the person he wanted to see. Why not? I had become so many fractals of myself—what was the harm in making up a new persona? Ellie Tsai I created for the girl I could have been.

Maybe I got carried away with the fun of it. Sure, eventually, the boys wanted to take me to lavish restaurants and give me gifts; who was I to say no? It was nice to experience wealth for once. I would return or resell the gifts for a sum and save for my future. Max's stepmom had a necklace she gave to me that was worth thousands. The start-up seed funding fell into my lap. And all it took was a clever lie. The lying was fun. Going out for a fancy dinner, just the two of us, where we could order the most expensive things on the menu, was fun. I realize now that the money part might have made you uncomfortable. Maybe you were jealous. For a while, I split it between us. We giddily spent money: on perfumes too expensive for us, on clothes, on a dinner that made us feel sick afterward because we'd ordered too much dessert. I'd promised to donate some of it to nonprofits of our choice, and you'd agreed. We were high school seniors on the cusp of becoming anyone.

We were in this together, Ingrid.

These are the secrets that you tried to twist away from me when you got scared. You hated when I started to enjoy it, and then you tried to saddle me with the blame. At first you thought scamming them was funny; later on, you said I was violating some moral code you'd made up. But what about when you convinced me to help you cheat on exams, or when you told me it would be a good idea to shoplift at the mall and you stayed tight-lipped when we got caught? Admit it: You only got jealous when I started living a better life than you. It was so clear, back then, that I would do anything for you. But you wouldn't do the same for me. You couldn't stand to be my sidekick.

By the time you told me to call the whole thing off, it was far too late. I couldn't come clean. I didn't want to. You could have stayed out of it. And yet you carefully planned my destruction.

I still remember this more clearly than anything. I'd finally confronted you about your birthday dinner after school one day in the empty auditorium. You didn't even look guilty or remorseful. You just looked at me with disgust and told me you didn't know the person I'd become, so why should you invite me to a dinner with the people who were the most special to you? That was when I realized that to you, our friendship was already over. Something you'd toss behind as senior year waned and you looked toward college.

And then you said: "You deserve to be locked up for what

you've done. If you don't come clean to them, I'll tell them myself."

All for something that was your idea to begin with.

You texted Max because you had his number from your internship, saying that you were giving him a tip that his girlfriend wasn't as she seemed. You told him to text the other boys. You planned on meeting them all at Dalton's party. I saw the screenshots on your phone, the texts you'd deleted on your end. You were going to make me out to be the sole orchestrator of this scheme. You were going to expose me to them all at once and set the three most powerful boys in La Jolla on me. On your best friend. Do you know what they could have done to me? How their families would have ruined mine? Could you imagine how it would break my mother?

They knew you were involved. After you were drugged, you probably blurted it out. And they thought you knew too much. Maybe that's when Max pushed you. Maybe he could tell that you were the one behind all this.

There are stories that we tell about ourselves. If you were determined to tell the truth, all I ever wanted to do was set it straight.

You'd know that what I told Jackie wasn't true.

Not that there wasn't a whistleblower at the company that got sued into oblivion—there was. We'd looked into that years ago and learned everything we could about it. But it wasn't my dad. He never worked for Bracken Pharma. The whistleblower was your dad's best friend. They'd moved away from La Jolla because of it.

You are the only person who knew what really happened to my dad.

Sixth grade, I came home from the school bus, straight toward the pantry because I knew I had tennis practice and only had ten minutes between when I arrived home and Mom would take me to the courts. If practice went well, I would ask Mom if I could go to yours that weekend for a sleepover, which I was pretty sure was going to happen. I was the best in the class, already long-limbed at eleven, taking after my dad in height. Ball handling, footwork: it all came naturally to me. But Mom wasn't grabbing her keys. She hadn't changed from her hotel clothes; she was picking up part-time shifts back then. And Dad was home, and there was a stack of papers and the laptop between them. Dad looked like he had shrunk, as if he were suddenly smaller than my mom. When I saw them, Dad opened his mouth to say something to me, but my mom stood up and stepped in front of him. I knew then that I wouldn't be going to tennis practice.

"Go upstairs," Mom said in this dazed, quiet tone. It alarmed me more than if she'd been shouting.

I stepped closer, trying to get a look at the papers. At first, I thought something was wrong with my dad. My mind flashed through the tragic possibilities. Cancer, some rare disease—that must have been the reason why he looked so despondent and lost. Dad pleaded, "Let me explain to her," and Mom cut him off. "No. You and I aren't done."

I went into my room and shut the door and I listened. I just remembered the questions my mom asked. Her voice rose until she was shouting and half-sobbing: *Who was this? How did you find her? How much? No, be honest with me; you owe me this. Just how much?*

That night, I'd gone to your house, and we'd put on *The Parent Trap*, and I told you that my parents were fighting and you comforted me.

The details came later: My dad had been chatting with a woman in an online forum for close to a year. What had originated as innocuous banter on a thread devolved into secret messaging apps. All these nights we'd thought my dad was staying up late to work, he'd been huddled in a conference room to talk to her into the night. She'd requested money in increasing sums, promising a life together once she came over to California. Then came the threat of the woman's husband, who'd found out and blackmailed my dad to not tell anyone. They probably were the same person. Later, I found out, my dad had sent close to $300,000.

Three hundred thousand fucking dollars. This amount I never told you, Ingrid. It would be years before I could understand the enormity of a number that sounded so fake. I now know how much that cost us. It was college, twice over. It was the ability to stay in our house. It was my parents getting to stay together, to show up to my graduation. It was my tennis lessons. I would never have the chance to be great at anything. But still, in that moment, staring at my bedroom ceiling and listening to my mother cry downstairs, I'd gotten the vague premonition, the realization that this was the end of my old life and the beginning of the rest of my life as I knew it.

But I'm being kind of selfish, talking just about myself. My dad's sweetheart scam ruined my life, but it obliterated my mother's. She'll never get that seaside cottage in La Jolla back. My dad moved out, and we moved into a small apartment. She took on more shifts at the hotel until she was working overtime every night because she worried about the cost of raising me, of protecting me. *It's just the two of us now*, she'd said to me. She'd never trust anyone again.

Don't you get it, Ingrid? No, you wouldn't. You teased me about daddy issues, dropped comments about me being so careful with money—and they hurt me, and I think you knew you could hurt me because you knew I wouldn't leave you. You saw me order appetizers as the main course at dinner and you laughed and asked me if I had an eating disorder. You know the broad strokes of the story but you don't know what it's like to hurtle through the changes that followed—the divorce, the selling of the house, the screaming fights, the eerie stillness once my dad left for good and my mom picked up extra night shifts at the hotel, until she became the manager on that shift. It was fucking humiliating. What my dad did wasn't just normal cheating. It was epic and colossal proportions of cheating, the kind you hear about on shitty Netflix shows and laugh at. *How could you have fallen for that?* I ask my dad that sometimes. I scream it at him in my head. I imagine seeing him again and I am at a loss for words, because what do I even say? I couldn't do anything at all. I could only watch as my family disintegrated. I watched my mom fold into the couch on her nights off, falling asleep to shows about grand old English manors, as if we would ever live in a house again.

You were the one who told me to stop playing a victim in my life and to make myself into the person I wanted to be.

Would you understand if I told you that I didn't want this to be the story that defined the rest of my life? Of course I jumped at the chance to leave it. This is what powered me; the desire to protect my best friend. And this dizzying, breathtaking kaleidoscope of possibilities that I could be, to walk around in the infinite and better versions of myself. If only—if only my dad didn't fuck up my life, this is what I could have aspired to be.

I was principled about it; I would only ever balance the scales. After your mom got laid off from Bracken, after Max stole your work, after I saw Dalton string you along and so cruelly dismiss you, I would only target the people who had made your life miserable. The heirs, who lived lives that wouldn't be damaged by thousands or even hundreds of thousands. Everything was fixed for them or secured to work for them. Nothing I did would ever make a dent; none of it would ever matter. It was cosmic retribution. And it was working. Getting the gifts and money was a side thing; after all, it couldn't hurt. I'd wreak emotional havoc on them for you before I would eventually break their hearts, and in the meantime, I'd get to support myself and my mom a little. It was working, and we would have gotten away with it all until you got nervous, until you got jealous when I decided I wasn't breaking up with Dalton after all, and you hated that I had something you didn't. You decided to punish me for it. You made the decision to ruin everything.

You didn't have to try to rat me out, you know. I told you—I was going to donate some of that money, anyway. But it didn't matter to you at the end. You said that it weighed on your conscience—what, to scam wealthy boys who lived in glass houses on the coast? You didn't tell me this, but I think you wanted Dalton for yourself. You wanted to turn me in so you could get close and have a chance with him.

I didn't mean for it all to happen the way it did; I hope you know that. I only spiked your drink at the party with Laurel Bracken's crushed-up benzos because I knew that those pills combined with booze would slow you down, make you confused, and make you so sleepy, you would pass out at Dalton's. I never thought you'd stumble your way to the cliffs and sloppily tell those boys the truth. I didn't even know you'd switched the meeting point to the cliffs. I didn't know exactly what was said there on that cliff, and now maybe I never will. Did Max threaten you? Were you scared for your life? Did the fall knock you unconscious, or were you in pain? There is a chance you could have been saved, and that is what breaks me. What I do know for a fact is that they abandoned you to the tide. They thought of themselves first, as they always do. And so they deserve what they got.

Unfortunately, I know how it's going to go: They're hiring the best defense lawyers in town. They're going to go for not guilty verdicts and get them. No consequences are going to touch them—the only thing that might linger is their own scattered remorse. What I did, though, was protect you. I told everyone you went to those boys because you were standing up for me. It makes you look like a hero, Ingrid. That's the memory they're always going to have of you.

Here on the cliffs where you died, it truly feels like I am alone, like I am at the edge of the earth, claimed and tethered by nothing. God, Ingrid. I wish it didn't all happen this way. We could have gone to college clutching this secret wild escapade between us, this one last elaborate senior prank, this one thing to tie us to each other. Instead, I'll be missing you for the rest of my life.

Chapter Twenty-Four

When I return to Jackie's house, her mom is making us coffee with sweetened condensed milk. I got flowers on the way home from the local farmers market, and her mom brightens when I give her the small bouquet of daisies. She loves me already. Jackie and I take her mom's new King Charles spaniel puppy out for a walk around the neighborhood and then grab pancakes at the breakfast diner. Everyone coos over the puppy, who falls asleep in my lap. We do the crossword together and then go to Warwick's. Jackie peruses the bookshelves, her eyebrows knit together, her lips slightly pursed. She looks up and the corners of her eyes crinkle. She grins right at me, raising an eyebrow, and I look away, embarrassed. The light beams softly down on her wavy dark hair, bringing out her highlights. She gets us ice cream on the way back to her house, and when we kiss, she tastes like sweet syrup. On the street, Jackie shrugs her tote bag full of new books I bought her over her shoulder, and she tells me, "So, my dad's thinking of going on a road trip to Joshua Tree this summer. You should come with."

"Really?" I ask. "You sure?"

Jackie tilts her head. "Of course. I want you to come. Please make it more bearable for me."

I pull her in. She's so short and cute. She has such an

intimidating presence that I actually forget she's quite small and that I can rest my chin on her head. The days ahead of us will be exhilarating and short-lived: two weeks of classes, then graduation. Jackie, of course, got the valedictorian title in the end, although these days it bothers me a lot less than it used to. We're both getting out of here and going where we wanted to.

Then the whole summer will stretch ahead of us. Jackie will be around, interning for the local newspaper. I'll be back working at the La Jolla Shores Beach Club, although working front office this go-around. Tutoring on the side, this time for real—turns out, acing all my APs and going to Berkeley does give me a bit of credibility in the neighborhood. We're hanging out later this week to watch a movie. At this point, I think we basically are going on dates. But neither of us has made a move to make things official. I want it to be, though.

When I finally arrive back to my apartment, it's early afternoon. Mom peers at me sleepily from the couch; the blue glow of the TV reflects in her glasses. She's dozing in the sun, and she seems content.

"Baobei. Did you have fun at prom?"

I nod. I walk over and kiss her on the top of her head. She smells like her Korean shampoo and something slightly bitter, maybe the herbal supplements she's been taking. And that jasmine scent of the hotel, as always.

She laughs. "You have glitter in your hair."

I sit next to her on the couch and she combs it out with her fingers while I think of how to ask Jackie to be my girlfriend. Maybe I'll make a crossword for her to spell out just that. She would love it.

"You seem so happy," my mom murmurs.

I lean back and grin with my eyes closed. She thinks Jackie and I have gone to the prom as friends. If we start to date, I think I will have to tell her. I don't know how she'll react, but I hope she'll be okay with it. I hope she can see how real it all is, how happy it makes me. And if I don't tell her, that's okay; it's not the worst secret I've kept.

"You know what you were saying, about moving to San Francisco?" I say. "I changed my mind. I think that's actually a great idea."

She looks up from my hair and beams. "Really?"

I lean down, draping my arms over her shoulders, and give her a big hug.

The money is secure in my bank account: $95,423.13, enough to pay for all of college, along with the financial aid I'm getting. Most of the money came from the payout from Peter Bracken, after I signed the NDA. I have a little bit of the money I've earned portioned away for my mother. It's nowhere near enough to buy a house, but I could help her rent a really nice apartment in San Francisco. I'll get her a beautiful table and new furniture that lasts, instead of things we've picked up from the curb. Art, too, maybe; a statement piece from an artist she admires. Her birthday is in a month. I'm going to write her a check that means she won't have to take out any loans. She'll finally get to be the architect she's dreamed of becoming. We all deserve to become the person we want to be, and no one is more deserving than my mother.

I go to Ingrid's GoFundMe memorial page and make an anonymous donation of $2,000.

And then I walk over to my room. I'm pretty sure I've deleted everything, all traces of evidence. The pills have long been ground into bits and flushed down the toilet. I log out of every account that isn't me. I abandon Amy Fang, Ellie Tsai, and Mia Leung, cast them out like phantoms to the sea. The lives I lived with them, the stories I could tell with those personas. But they were always meant to be fictional. Eventually, I am just me again: Amelia Wu. For the first time, I'm not focused on who else to become. I like who I am right now.

Epilogue
Jackie Anh

I think there is a special theory of relativity for when you just get into a relationship. The first two months of summer fly by incomprehensibly fast with Amelia Wu. My days are full working at *The San Diego Union-Tribune*. They don't usually allow high school interns, but I was able to convince them during my interview process and with some stellar recommendation letters from my teachers. The college interns underestimate me, of course. I outshine all of them until I'm put on the interesting stories. After I leave work, though, I go to meet Amelia by the beach, where she is just getting off her shift. Sometimes one of us brings food; sometimes we just sit on the rocks. We watch the sunset, and I glance over. I can't help staring, and she usually catches me and gives me a teasing look before she kisses me.

She is such a good kisser.

Weeks pass like this. There are planned dates and farmers market runs and movie nights and even more picnics on the beach. I schedule dates on her Google Calendar all the way through the end of the year. I'm determined for us to survive the long distance (even though the miles between Berkeley and Stanford hardly qualify as *distance* at all). A lot of high school relationships fall apart before or in college. I know ours won't.

My mom loves her and invites her over for dinner all the time. There's a weekend in Joshua Tree with my dad and his now fiancée, which annoys me slightly less because I get to be with Amelia. We go off on our little hikes, and I show her rocks in the stream and tell her about geological formations. She calls me the biggest nerd she's ever encountered and yet her hand slips into mine and squeezes it, so I guess being into rocks gets you some action after all. At nighttime the temperature drops in the desert, and she huddles in her sleeping bag next to mine and we point out stars together, and it's possible I have never been happier. We get back, and suddenly it's late July and she and her mom are preparing to move out of their apartment. I spend whatever free time I can helping them pack things into their boxes. She leaves and I go to the beach alone that day and cry for an hour straight, missing her. I try to be pragmatic about it. I'll only miss her during the holidays, when I'm back in San Diego. The rest of the year we'll be in basically the same place.

Without her, the latter half of the summer drags to a standstill. It doesn't help that my internship ends the week after she leaves. I'm on the quarter system, which means that I start in late September, so I need to find a way to kill time for almost five weeks. The first day, I have nothing to do and end up scouring the map of Stanford's campus and researching the student ratings of the professors of the prospective classes I want to take.

I set up a coffee chat with the current editor in chief of *The Stanford Daily* on Instagram, who currently has a postgrad one-year fellowship at *The New York Times* lined up, but even that still leaves me with too much time on my hands.

Which is how I come up with my own project for myself. I'm going to investigate the whistleblower case and expose Bracken Pharmaceuticals once and for all. This case has nagged at me ever since Amelia told me about it. She's changed the subject every time I've brought it up to her, which is very understandable. She's likely traumatized and doesn't want to hear of anything related to that company again. Especially after Max Bracken almost killed her and then got off easy with probation and a six-week mandatory alcohol and drug disorder program. I want to seek revenge on the entire company. Clandestine levels of cover-up, a potential health care crisis—this is huge prime-time news and I have to get to the bottom of it. This will be John Carreyrou levels of journalism. It gives me chills just thinking about it. When I move to Stanford and visit her in two months—we already have a date planned in San Francisco—I will get to show her all the information I was able to gather. She won't even have to worry about searching for the facts herself. I'll do it all for her. I'll shield her from any involvement in this research effort.

I work quickly. Within days I have contacts from LinkedIn lined up to speak with me. In fact, one of them is calling me right now. The area code is 713. From Texas.

"Hi, this is Jacqueline Anh," I say. "Is this Daniel Severs?"

"This is."

"Hi, Daniel." I pull up my questions. "Thank you so much for taking the time to speak with me today and for answering my email. I want you to know that this entire conversation is off the record, and so you can feel free to speak at will. With that said, I'd like to ask about the whistleblower case on Bracken Pharmaceuticals six years ago, regarding the heart medication Paloxene. What was your relationship with Lin Wu?"

"Lin Wu? Who is Lin Wu?"

I falter. "The whistleblower?"

"No, I never worked with a Lin Wu, I can tell you that much," Daniel says emphatically. "If you're talking about the Paloxene case, my coworker's name was Nazek Arbajian. And I can't speak too much about him. This was ten years ago. Sorry. I thought this call was about the specifics of the drug itself, not the controversy. You're better off finding someone else."

There is a beep and the line goes dead.

I lean back in my desk chair. This doesn't make sense. Do I have Amelia's dad's name wrong? And how did this happen ten years ago when Amelia said her dad left their family when she was ten? Do I have the details entirely wrong? He seemed so confident, and he has no reason to lie . . .

But what if Amelia is?

That thought punctures my mind with such force, it surprises me. She's my girlfriend. She loves me; she told me and me alone the truth. She trusts me, and I, her. I still remember everything about the afternoon we sat in her car together outside Bracken. How she spoke with such earnestness and pain. How can I doubt her?

There's only one way to find out. The rest of the summer unfolds before me, weeks and weeks of it. I turn to my computer and start doing what I do best: I begin to dig.

# Acknowledgments

This book would not be the book it is or exist at all without the enduring support I received during this writing process.

To Jess, agent extraordinaire, for always being in my corner for the past decade. I can never thank you enough.

To Elizabeth and Alex, my wonderful and brilliant editors, for your steady guidance, for your enthusiasm, and for many fun, fruitful, and wild plot brainstorming sessions.

To the Penguin Workshop team: Jay Emmanuel, Brandy Colbert, Caroline Press, Monica White, and Rima Weinberg, thank you so much.

To Joelle and Racquel, for witnessing the origin of this book at that house on the Ireland coast. I'm overflowing with gratitude and admiration for you both. Thank you for being my confidantes and steady anchors in writing and life.

To my dearest d.a.c.u—Chloe, Racquel (again), Tashie, Zoe: I would be nothing and nowhere without you all, my loves. Thank you for the hand-holding, the safe haven, and the sprawling lore.

To Katia, for being my twin mind and the greatest childhood best friend. I have become a better self in every way because of you.

To my family. To Justin, for reading each of my books. To my parents for their support. To Yuk, Ophelia, Tim, Lil, Bella, Julie.

To Katherine, for the generous fact-checks (and to Simba!). To Lauren, for the endless laughs and chats.

To Andi, for your kindness and wisdom, for introducing me to *The Traitors*, and for the Princess Writing Retreat. To Sean, for the humor and tech save in my hour of need.

To my beloved Squirrels: Cate, Eghosa, Gaby. To Becca, Rachel, Pranavi, Marilyn, Elaine, Adrienne, Katie, Vida, Grace, Camryn, Jake, Michael W., Fari, Pietra, Kei, Squish, Abbie, Gracie, Kamilah, Audrey, Anna, Lexi, Therese, Aamna, Fiona, Lily, Dan, Michael E., Dave, Paula.

And lastly, thank you to librarians, booksellers, educators, and readers, for the enthusiasm and for the inimitable and tireless work you do. I would be nowhere without you.